The kiss had done funny things to her body

Jessie tried to blame those *funny things* on the pregnancy, but she knew it wasn't her condition causing it. This was some kind of spooky attraction to a man she knew she shouldn't be attracted to. There was just one problem. She didn't know how to make it stop.

"Are you all right?"

She didn't realize she'd been staring at him. And there was certainly a lot of him to stare at. Jeans, worn white in places she wished weren't so obvious. A blue cotton shirt that showed nearly every muscle the man had.

"Have you felt the baby move?" He reached out and placed his hand over her abdomen. It was probably a mistake, but she looked at him again. Their gazes met. Held. That unwavering, almost pleading look in his eyes caused her breath to stall in her throat.

It was his child....

Dear Harlequin Intrigue Reader,

Welcome to a brand-new year of exciting romance and edge-of-your-seat suspense. We at Harlequin Intrigue are thrilled to renew our commitment to you, our loyal readers, to provide variety and outstanding romantic suspense—each and every month.

To get things started right, veteran Harlequin Intrigue author Cassie Miles kicks off a two-book miniseries with *State of Emergency*. The COLORADO SEARCH AND RESCUE group features tough emergency personnel reared in the shadows of the rugged Rocky Mountains. Who wouldn't want to be stranded with a western-born hunk trained to protect and serve?

Speaking of hunks, Debra Webb serves up a giant of a man in *Solitary Soldier*, the next installment in her COLBY AGENCY series. And you know what they say about the bigger they come the harder they fall....Well, it goes double for this wounded hero.

Ann Voss Peterson takes us to the darkest part of a serial killer's world in *Accessory to Marriage*. The second time around could prove to be the last—permanently—for both the hero and heroine in this gripping thriller.

Finally, please welcome Delores Fossen to the line. She joins us with a moving story of forced artificial insemination, which unites two strangers who unwittingly become parents...and eventually a family. Do not miss *His Child* for an emotional read.

Be sure to let us know how we're doing; we love to hear from our readers! And Happy New Year from all of us at Harlequin Intrigue.

Sincerely,

Denise O'Sullivan
Associate Senior Editor
Harlequin Intrigue

HIS CHILD
DELORES FOSSEN

HARLEQUIN®

TORONTO • NEW YORK • LONDON
AMSTERDAM • PARIS • SYDNEY • HAMBURG
STOCKHOLM • ATHENS • TOKYO • MILAN • MADRID
PRAGUE • WARSAW • BUDAPEST • AUCKLAND

ISBN 0-373-22648-9

HIS CHILD

ABOUT THE AUTHOR

Imagine a family tree that includes Texas cowboys, Choctaw and Cherokee Indians, a Louisiana pirate and a Scottish rebel who battled side by side with William Wallace. With ancestors like that, it's easy to understand why Texas author and former air force captain Delores Fossen feels as if she was genetically predisposed to writing romances. Along the way to fulfilling her DNA destiny, Delores married an air force Top Gun who just happens to be of Viking descent. With all those romantic bases covered, she doesn't have to look too far for inspiration.

Books by Delores Fossen

HARLEQUIN INTRIGUE
648—HIS CHILD

Don't miss any of our special offers. Write to us at the following address for information on our newest releases.

Harlequin Reader Service
U.S.: 3010 Walden Ave., P.O. Box 1325, Buffalo, NY 14269
Canadian: P.O. Box 609, Fort Erie, Ont. L2A 5X3

CAST OF CHARACTERS

Jessie Barrett—Someone wants her dead. Jessie's only hope is Jake McClendon—the biological father of her unborn child. But will the prominent Texas rancher help a woman he's never even met?

Jake McClendon—Texas rancher turned politician. Could he trust Jessie—the mother of a child he desperately wants, but thought he could never have?

Abel Markham—Jake's political opponent. A man with more ambition than ethics.

Douglas Harland—Jake's brother-in-law and campaign manager. He wants nothing—including Jessie—getting in the way of the campaign.

Willa Harland—Jake's socialite sister. Is she overly protective of her brother—or does she have a different reason for wanting Jessie out of his life?

Detective Byron DuCiel—Jessie's best friend. Does he have his own personal agenda, or is he truly trying to help Jessie?

To my husband, Colonel Thomas Fossen,
who encourages me, inspires me
and makes sure I keep my sense of wonder.

Chapter One

Jessie hid in the shadows and waited for him. By now, Jake McClendon probably thought she was dead. He wouldn't be expecting her or the Saturday Night Special she had gripped in her hands.

He was in for a real surprise.

Not only was she still alive, she was here, armed and in his hotel suite. No guards or restraints to stop her now. One way or another, she would get answers.

The doorknob rattled, and she heard voices in the hall. So he wasn't alone. Sweet heaven, could nothing go right? Jessie softly groaned and ducked behind the thick brocade drapes. She'd still be able to see him by looking in the mirror over the fireplace, but she wouldn't confront him until the other person left. Best not to draw anyone else into this.

Pulling in a hard breath, she leaned back against the cool glass of the balcony door. It didn't ease the throbbing in her head, nor did it loosen the muscles that burned in her shoulders and back. Her body was a tangle of nerves and spent adrenaline. The bone-weary fatigue didn't help, either. She'd been fighting off the effects of exhaustion for hours now.

Or had it been days?

God, she didn't even know how long it had been since she managed to escape from that warehouse. For that matter, she had no idea how long they had held her captive. All she knew was that the person responsible was about to come through that door. He would answer for what he'd done to her.

"It wasn't smart to insult him." The man pushed open the door and issued that crisp remark over his shoulder. "You need him and his clout."

Glancing at his reflection in the mirror, she saw his blond hair. Definitely not Jake McClendon. McClendon's photographs were standard fare in the local newspapers. There was no shortage of publicity shots for the Lone Star State's golden boy and congressional candidate.

McClendon walked in behind the other man. "I can do without that kind of clout." He had already removed the tux jacket and was working on the tie. He tugged at it as if it were fighting back.

Jessie's eyes narrowed. Finally. She was in the same room with the man who wanted her dead.

"You're wrong." The blond man again. His name was Douglas Harland, Jessie remembered, and he was married to McClendon's sister. "You need Emmett."

"And how about his wife?" McClendon tossed the jacket onto the sofa and shoved a hand through his short coffee-colored hair. "Do I need her, too? She thinks a campaign contribution obligates me to sleep with her."

"So? Consider it stud service." The corner of Douglas's mouth hitched. "You knew there'd be things about this campaign you wouldn't like."

"I don't like any part of it." McClendon shrugged

and undid the top buttons of his shirt. "I want to be in the Texas Legislature. That doesn't mean I want to sleep my way there."

McClendon moved to the fireplace, just beneath the mirror, where Jessie could easily see his face. A face that reflected none of the evil inside him. Deeply tanned skin. Sharp angled cheekbones, a legacy from his Comanche grandmother—something the press often mentioned. His brows slanted downward, making his expression a natural frown. His mouth was rigid. But not stern. Under different circumstances she might have considered him good-looking. Even handsome.

But it wasn't different circumstances.

McClendon was the enemy, in every sense of the word.

He was taller than she'd expected. Over six feet. Lean. Built like the cowboy he was underneath the polished elegance of the tux. A real wolf in sheep's clothing.

"You'll just have to accept this stud status of yours," Douglas continued, a hint of amusement in his voice. "Women want to heal your wounds because you're a widower. It's a chick thing." He glanced down at his watch. "We need to get back before we're missed."

It seemed as if he was about to answer, but then McClendon went still. Perfectly still. And much to Jessie's horror, he looked straight in the mirror. She tried not to move a muscle, even though he would probably see her reflection if he glanced at the curtains.

"Go ahead back to the party," he finally said. "I'll be down soon. I just need to make a few calls."

Jessie allowed herself a quiet breath of relief. So, he hadn't seen her. She wouldn't have to reveal her hand while the other man was still in the room.

Before Douglas Harland even issued a "don't be long" and closed the door behind him, McClendon went to the bar and poured himself a drink. He took the shot in one gulp, then slapped down the glass. In the same motion, he tipped his head toward the curtain. "Mind telling me what you're doing behind there?"

Jessie went board stiff. There had been nothing in his body language to indicate he'd noticed her.

"Well?" he snarled. "I'm waiting."

She stepped out, using her forearm to push the curtain aside so she wouldn't have to lower the gun. For a moment she just stood there and sized him up. Jessie swallowed hard. In a hand-to-hand battle, she would lose. Big time. It wasn't just his size; it was his street-wise expression. He'd won his share of fights. More, no doubt, than she had.

"How did you know I was here?" Jessie asked.

"Lucky guess," he said, sardonically enough for her to understand that he had indeed seen her in the mirror. "What do you plan to do with that gun?"

Jessie glanced at it and then him. "It's my insurance. To make sure you listen to what I have to say."

"Then, by all means go on—say it. Then get the hell out of here before my brother-in-law comes back to check on me."

Yes, him. Jessie hadn't considered that he might come back anytime soon. But she should have. She should have anticipated all the contingencies. She cursed the fog in her head. Because of it, she was already a step behind him.

There seemed to be nothing wrong with Mc-Clendon's thought processes, however. His laser-blue eyes were clear and trained right on her. He seemed ready to strike.

"I want some answers." She fought back a sudden wave of dizziness. Effects of the fatigue, maybe. And maybe something else. Jessie prayed she could stay strong long enough to finish this.

"So do I. I'd say I'm entitled to some, since you're holding a gun on me. For starters, do I even know you?"

"I have reason to believe you do."

"You want money, is that it?" he asked.

A soft burst of air left her mouth. Almost a laugh, but it was lathered with sarcasm. "Money doesn't solve everything. Why did you have them come after me like that? Why me?"

"Why did I have them come after you? I don't know what you're talking about, lady. I've never seen you before."

"You didn't have to see me to give the order for them to pick me up and take me to that warehouse."

"Them?" He leaned against the bar and folded his arms over his chest. "Exactly who are you talking about?"

How dare he pull this act with her. "You know. You darn well know!"

"I don't know, and you've got about five seconds to start explaining, before I call the cops."

She waved the pistol, in case he'd forgotten that she was in charge here. For a man being held at gunpoint, he didn't seem threatened or even nervous. She, on the other hand, was shaking, and her stomach was clenched tight. "There will be some explanations, and they'll come from you. Why?"

"Why what?"

Jessie gave a frustrated groan. "Why me? Why did you have them do this to me? Why did you tell them to use me like that?"

"If you'll tell me what you *think* I had *them* do to you, then maybe I can help you clear this up."

"Why did you give the order for them to kill me and do those other things? Why would you want this to happen?" She shook her head in disgust. "What you had them do was sick."

"Back up some. Who wants to kill you?"

Jessie frowned. "You!"

"Not me. Who?"

"Your hired help, then. Three men and a woman. I never saw their faces, but they chloroformed me and took me to that warehouse. They held me for, uh—what's the date?"

He didn't look as if he intended to answer her. He just stood there, the picture of intimidation. "It's July sixteenth," he finally said.

"July?" How could that be? Jessie pressed her fingertips against her temple, and her bottom lip started to tremble. She'd seen the date on the newspaper, of course, but it hadn't registered until now. Suddenly, it all became much clearer. "Three months. They took me back in April."

He shrugged. "And what exactly do you think these people did to you during these three months?"

"Things. And now I think I might be…" But the word stuck like wet clay in her throat.

"What? Lady, will you just spit this out so I can

get you out of here?'' he demanded. "What might
you be?''

"Pregnant." It left her mouth on a gasp. The room
started to whirl in a black circle. Jessie leaned against
the balcony door and let it support her.

"Pregnant,'' he spat out, in the same way he did
the profanity he uttered next. "This sounds like a
personal problem to me. Why would you hold me at
gunpoint just to tell me you're pregnant?''

"Because—" She grabbed the drapes, but it didn't
stop her from sinking to her knees. The plush carpet
broke her fall, some. "It's your baby.''

LIKE HELL IT WAS.

Jake was one-hundred percent sure of that. He
hadn't been with a woman, any woman, in nearly a
year. She was obviously some kind of strung-out nut.
A stalker maybe. And definitely mentally unstable.
There was no way he could be the father of her child,
assuming she was even pregnant. That, too, could be
the product of her drug-induced imagination.

Now he just had to figure out what to do with her.

Jake reached for the phone to call the police. Then
stopped. He looked at her. Really looked at her. It
was easier to do now, since she no longer had the
gun pointed at him. He'd taken that from her as soon
as she fainted. He had also moved her to the sofa.
Why, he didn't know. He should have gotten her out
of there as quickly as possible. He should have
turned this over already to the police.

He should have.

But for some reason, he hadn't.

She wore an ill-fitting maid's uniform that was
several sizes too big for her rail-thin body. Obvi-

ously, the garment was something she'd stolen. Jake pushed her badly cut, midnight-colored hair away from her face and tried to remember if he'd seen her before.

Nothing about her seemed familiar. Absolutely nothing.

He'd never had sex with her—that was for sure. Since his wife's death, there had been only a few women. Rare encounters that he could definitely count on one hand. She wasn't one of those encounters.

Despite the clothes and the bad haircut, she was pretty. Well, she would have been if she hadn't looked so ill. Her skin was pale, like skim milk. It emphasized the sprinkling of freckles on her slim nose. Maybe she wasn't just strung-out, but sick. The bruise-colored smudges under her eyes and her parched lips said loads about her health. Or, if she hadn't lied about her condition, then maybe the pregnancy had taken its toll.

Still, it was no skin off his hide. So what if the woman was pregnant?

It's your baby.

No way was that humanly possible. Boy, had she picked the wrong guy to try to pin this on.

She stirred, moaning softly, and touched her fingertips to her forehead. Slowly, her eyelids fluttered open. She squinted. Then, groaned. "No. Please not this. Stupid. Stupid. Stupid."

Jake frowned. She had to be talking about herself. Not him. He hadn't decided if she was actually stupid. Or maybe she was just crazy. He intended to find out soon enough.

"How long before the cops get here?" she asked.

"I haven't called them yet." He shoved his hands in his pockets and stared down at her. "Let me tell you how this is going to work. I'll ask the questions, and you'll answer them. If the answers please me, I won't call the cops at all."

Wincing and mumbling, she sat up and scrubbed her hands over her face. "You'll just kill me, then."

Well, she was definitely crazy. "Right. Lady, I'm a congressional candidate, not a hired gun. No, I won't kill you."

"Then, what else could you possibly do to me that you haven't done already?"

There was some fight left in her last question, making Jake rethink the sick theory. She was down but not out. Somehow, it made it easier for him to confront her. He hated to kick someone when they were down.

"I can have you arrested—that's what I can do," he informed her. "I think a breaking and entering charge and possession of a firearm will put you away for a while, don't you?"

She ran her fingers through her hair. "Like I care about those piddly charges, when you want me dead. Why? Why did you have them do this and then order a hit on me?"

"Oh, no. We're not going down that road again. I haven't done anything to you—especially get you pregnant and order a hit on you. Now let's go back to the part about me asking the questions and you answering them. For starters, exactly who the heck are you?"

"Jessie—"

She boldly met his gaze. Her eyes were the color of a gun barrel. Steely gray and just as hard.

"But you already know that."

"Uh-uh. Don't start that again. If I knew, I wouldn't have asked. What's your full name?"

"Jessie...Smith."

He made an annoying sound like the buzzer on a game show. "Wrong answer. Try again."

A muscle flickered in her sleek jaw. "Briggs."

He didn't believe her, but at least he had something to work with. It was certainly better than calling her *lady*. She was anything but a lady. "All right, Jessie Briggs, tell me why you think I'm trying to kill you."

"I don't know why, but you ordered those people to kidnap me."

"People," Jake flatly repeated. "The three men and the woman you mentioned? The ones who held you for three months?"

She nodded. "But you're the one who hired them to take me to that warehouse. You had them use me, and—"

"Hold it right there. That's the part I want to talk about now. Exactly how did they use you?"

She made a sound of outrage and bolted to her feet as if ready to tear out of the room. But she didn't go anywhere. She pressed both hands to the sides of her head and sagged back down to the sofa.

"Dizzy?" he asked.

She tossed him a *you think?* look. "I guess it's just one of the little joys of my condition."

"Well, I suppose it's time we broached that subject. Would you like to explain exactly how you think I got you pregnant? Afterward, I can blow anything you say right out of the water."

"They inseminated me." She didn't even hesitate. "On your orders, I'm sure."

Jake froze. That wasn't the answer he wanted to hear. All right, so he couldn't blow anything out of the water just yet. He had to think about that for a moment. Then he discounted it. "That's impossible."

"No, it's not. I'll spare you the exact details of how they did it, but I know what happened to me. And so do you."

He paused, reconsidered it. But discounted it again just as fast. There were holes a mile wide in her story. "Let's suppose for a minute that someone did inseminate you. What makes you think I was involved in any way?"

Again, she didn't hesitate. "Your name was on the vial they took out of that weird bucket. I saw it. I don't think they meant for me to, but I did. They'd given me a drug, and I guess they thought I was unconscious. I wasn't. Plus, I heard them mention your name."

Yes, in her dreams she'd probably heard someone mention his name. "This is a real cartload of bull you're telling me, Miss Briggs. What I can't believe is that you had the nerve to come here with it."

"Are you saying you don't have semen stored somewhere?"

"That's *exactly* what I'm saying."

"At Cryogen Labs right here in San Antonio," she clarified. "That's what it said on the vial, along with your name and the numbers 6837. I'm not an idiot, Mr. McClendon. I've read about your Hodgkin's disease. I know you stored semen before you went into therapy. Do you deny that?"

So, she did know about his illness six years ago. It didn't make him believe her story. It just meant she'd done her homework. "I don't deny it, but what you couldn't have read in the newspaper was that my vials were accidentally destroyed nearly four months ago. Only a handful of people know that." He paused so she could grasp that. "Would you like to leave on your own, or do I need to toss you out of here myself?"

Her eyes widened for a second, and then narrowed just as quickly. "The number on the vial was 6837. Call Cryogen Labs and see if that matches what they say was destroyed."

Oh, she was good. Really good. Coming up with the number of the vial was a nice touch, but it wouldn't make him believe her. "I'll call them in a minute—but first I have another question. Hypothetically speaking, let's say someone did inseminate you. You're sure you became pregnant?"

"I heard them say so, yes. I didn't see the test results, but I'm having some symptoms that make me think they succeeded in what you wanted them to do."

"You said they drugged you. Your symptoms could be from that."

Her eyebrow rose sharply. "Not these symptoms. And they didn't keep me drugged all the time, just locked up. They only drugged me when they did those, uh, procedures on me."

He didn't want to delve into that any further, not when he had so many other things to discuss. "Another hypothetical question, then. Why would anyone want to do this?"

"That's what I want you to answer. Trust me, I've

been giving it a lot of thought. Maybe you wanted some surrogate mother and you didn't want to go through the hassle of doing it the legal way.''

He shook his head. ''That doesn't make sense.''

''It does if you didn't want the publicity because of your campaign. Some people are opposed to surrogate pregnancies. You probably didn't want to risk offending any ultra-conservative voters. This way, you could adopt the child and pretend you're still a good guy who's giving some orphan a chance to be raised by a millionaire rancher-turned-congressman. You're the winner all the way around.''

Jake still didn't believe her story, and that theory was just plain asinine, but he could definitely see this from a different angle. A much different angle. If, and that was a Texas-sized if, there was any truth to what this woman said, it could be a plot by someone out to get him. Suppose someone wanted to use the child to embarrass him or to hurt his campaign? Even in this day and age, conservative voters wouldn't care much for a future congressman having an illegitimate child.

She raked her tongue over her bottom lip. ''But something must have gone wrong, because I heard them say they were going to kill me. Thank God I was able to escape before they could get around to doing that.''

''They said they were going to kill you?'' Jake repeated. ''Well, that shoots holes in your surrogate mom theory, huh? Why would I go through all that trouble to inseminate you, and then kill you before I even knew for sure if you're pregnant?''

''I don't know. I told you, that's why I'm here. I need answers.''

"Well, you came to the wrong place, lady. Let me correct that, you came to the wrong *man*. I'm not buying any of this, so why don't we just cut to the chase and you spit out exactly what you want. Money up front? Or are you doing this for blackmail so you can drag out the payments for years? Because either way I don't intend to give you a dime."

She tipped her head to the phone. "Make the call to Cryogen Labs. Vial number 6837."

Jake looked at the phone, and then her. "All right, I will." It was about time he called her bluff. He walked across the room, using the mirror to keep an eye on her. "I don't suppose you know their phone number?"

"No."

"No," he mimicked sarcastically under his breath.

Jake didn't know what to make of that. A con artist would have known the number. A victim of the crime she'd just described wouldn't. Of course, she could be a very good con artist who was pretending she didn't know. There was only one way to find out.

He got the number from directory assistance and called the lab. Jake wasn't even sure the place would be open, but someone picked up on the third ring.

"This is Jake McClendon. I wanted to verify some information about specimens I had stored there." The woman who answered the call asked him to provide some identifying data. Once that was out of the way, he got down to business. "I need to know about the six vials I had in Cryogen Labs. I want to make sure they were indeed destroyed."

"Oh, yes, they were, Mr. McClendon. Didn't someone contact you about it?"

"They did." He glanced at Jessie. She stepped closer and stared at him. Her eyes darkened like storm clouds. "Equipment failure, the person said."

"I'm afraid all the samples in that particular tank were destroyed. You are eligible for compensation from our insurance carrier."

He wasn't interested in insurance. In fact, before today Jake hadn't been interested in the vials at all. He'd stored them at Cryogen in case the treatment for his Hodgkin's Disease left him sterile. Since it hadn't, he had forgotten they even existed. Until he got that call four months ago.

"I need the vial numbers," he explained to the woman.

"Certainly. I have that right here in the computer."

He heard the clicking of her fingers on the keys, and made another spot-check on Jessie. Now she was looking around the room. For her gun, no doubt. She wouldn't find it. Jake had wrapped it in a plastic dry cleaner's bag and put it in the closet in the bedroom. Later, he wanted someone to check the weapon for fingerprints. That was probably the only way he would find out who she really was.

"Okay, here we are," the woman finally said. "The vials were numbered consecutively from 6851 through 6855. As I said, they were all destroyed."

So, there was no 6837. But Jessie Briggs had been damn close. Jake was about to end the call and confront his visitor, when he realized the numbers that the woman gave him only accounted for five vials.

"There were six specimens," he pointed out.

"Oh, yes. I see what happened. The first vial was the one you originally gave us. The other five were collected later at your physician's office and then transferred here.''

''And the number on that first vial?''

''Let's see. That would have been 6837.''

The muscles tightened in his chest. Jake refused to allow himself to react beyond that. This meant nothing. There was a reasonable explanation. All he had to do was find it. ''And where is that vial?'' he asked.

''I'm afraid it was destroyed also.''

Not according to the woman in his hotel suite. But then, she was obviously a liar. Her story didn't make a lick of sense. Nobody in his or her right mind would kidnap a woman, inseminate her and then try to kill her. Would they?

No. They wouldn't.

He hung up the phone to confront his lying visitor. There was just one problem.

She wasn't there.

And the door to his suite was wide open.

Chapter Two

Adjusting the plastic bag of groceries, Jessie cradled the phone against her shoulder and pushed the coins into the slot. Someone had scratched crude profanity into the black plastic box, and the mouthpiece smelled like dog's breath. The phone company would not have been pleased. It didn't exactly please her, either. She tried not to breathe too deeply, knowing the smell would turn her stomach.

She entered the numbers and waited. Not long. As she'd expected, he answered almost immediately. "Detective DuCiel."

"Byron, it's me." Jessie tried to keep her vigilant gaze on everything going on around her. It was rush hour. A little past five o'clock. The traffic crawled down St. Mary's Street. Horns honked. People hurried on the sidewalk. There was enough activity for her to get lost in the crowd, and she counted heavily on it. Getting lost was the only thing that made sense right now.

"Well, it's about time you called. You said I might not hear from you for months, but I didn't believe it." The relief in Byron's voice soon turned to a bark. "Where the heck are you, anyway? What happened? I was ready to—"

"I only have a few seconds. It isn't safe to talk here." It probably wasn't safe anywhere, but Jessie didn't say that.

"Where are you? I'll come right now."

"That wouldn't be smart, for either of us. I just wanted you to know that I'm—" What? Not *all right*. She wasn't all right by a long shot. "Alive," she finished. "I'm alive." And terrified. She wouldn't mention that, either, even though Byron would almost certainly hear it in her voice.

"That, I can figure out myself. Why the heck haven't you called me before now? Jess, it's been three months."

"It's a long story. Too long to get into here. I'm not sure what's going on."

"It's about Christy, isn't it."

Just the mention of her friend's name made Jessie's heart feel tight and heavy. It was as if a fist had gripped it and wouldn't let go. Christy had been dead eight months, and the pain was still just as fresh, just as raw as it had been when Byron had come by the apartment to tell her the news. The news that Christy wouldn't be coming home, ever.

It was so strange. Even though she'd seen her friend's body, it was still hard to believe Christy was dead. It was hard to believe Jessie would never again hear the laughter that had come so easily to the fun-loving woman that she considered a sister in every way that counted.

"You were asking too many questions about Christy's death," Byron concluded. "And someone didn't like it."

Maybe. And maybe it had nothing to do with Christy. Jessie just didn't know. She didn't have time to speculate out here in the open, where she was a sitting duck. That didn't mean she was giving up on finding the person responsible for Christy's death. She would *never* do that. One way or another, she would get to the bottom of it. It was a promise she'd sworn to Christy, and herself, the day of the funeral.

She pushed the painful memories away, knowing she couldn't deal with them at the moment. "Listen, Byron, I can't talk much longer. I need some money, but I'm afraid I'll be spotted. I want you to do it the way we talked about before I left Austin. Transfer all of it."

"All of it? Jess, what's wrong? Let me come and get you right now. Or better yet, go to the nearest police station."

Jessie ignored that advice. "Please do the money transfer and work out some travel arrangements. I need to disappear for a while. It'll take—what? Two days? Three?"

"If I do it the way you wanted, it'll take three. I'll have to cover my tracks."

She didn't tell him how much that scared her. Three days of hiding out. Three days of praying they wouldn't find her again. "I'll pick up the money at the location we discussed. I also need you to check out a warehouse here in San Antonio. And be careful. I don't know the exact address, but it's on Isom Road, near the airport. It's sandwiched between two old brownstone buildings."

"What happened there?" he asked. "Why do you want me to check it out?"

"Just see if you find anything unusual—but don't

go in there alone, Byron. It might not be safe. Also, I'd like for you to lean a little on my former employer, Ray Galindo. See if anyone was asking about me at the cantina before I disappeared. I'll call you again when I can.''

"No!'' Byron shouted. "Talk to me now. Go to the local cops—''

"I can't do that. If I tell them everything, you'll be in a lot of trouble.''

"To heck with that. You go to the cops. You get yourself some protection.''

"Maybe—''

"There are no 'maybes' about it.''

Jessie took a deep breath. "All right. I'll go to the San Antonio police, just as soon as I have the money.'' And maybe during those three days, she could figure out exactly why someone wanted her dead. "I don't want to put my neck out that far unless I have some way to hide afterward.''

She hung up the phone, ignoring the shouts and profanity from the one person she considered her friend.

Jessie didn't know what was going on, but she wouldn't bring Byron into this. Not yet. It definitely wasn't the right time to tell the San Antonio police, either. She didn't believe they could stop what Jake McClendon and his hired help had already put into motion. They couldn't save her. She was on somebody's hit list, and all the cops in the state of Texas probably couldn't stop it.

Jessie pulled the black Spurs cap lower on her forehead and started toward the motel. Such as it was. She had been able to retrieve some money—the cash from a locker she'd rented at a bowling alley.

But staying at a more comfortable place might put the wrong people back on her trail. That's why she'd chosen the downtown area, and not the north side where the kidnappers had originally found her. Maybe, just maybe, the change of location would help keep her alive.

The accommodations didn't matter much to her, anyway, and they were temporary. In three days she would have to leave San Antonio. No doubt about it. Staying would be a mistake, and she'd made too many of those already.

One of the biggest mistakes had been going to Jake McClendon's hotel. Now that she'd shaken off some of the effects of the fatigue and adrenaline, she wondered what had possessed her to do something that incredibly stupid. Breaking into a suite in one of the ritziest hotels on the San Antonio Riverwalk. Holding a gun on a man like him. And with all those risks, she hadn't accomplished a darn thing—something she should have realized in advance.

What had she expected him to do? Admit to everything? Yeah, right.

Instead, she should have spent that time trying to figure out why all of this had happened to her. Of course, two days of thinking about it hadn't produced any answers—but eventually something had to make sense. The surrogate pregnancy plot was still her first bet, if she could just figure out why McClendon had changed his mind and decided to kill her, instead.

She checked for the small dot of lipstick on the doorknob of her motel room. Still there, and in the same spot, to indicate the knob hadn't been touched. It was an inexpensive way to detect intruders, but it wasn't the only thing she'd added. The small door alarm she had purchased from a discount store hadn't been tripped. Once inside, she closed the door and quickly reset the alarm.

Jessie turned on the lights and set the groceries on the foot-wide counter of the kitchenette. In this case, the kitchenette consisted of a broken microwave oven, a small fridge, and a counter with a warped top.

Home, sweet home.

A dump, actually. It was a lot like the places she'd lived as a kid. The once-white paint on the walls was now dingy yellow. Shag carpet. A shade of green no one made anymore, or wanted. The shag had been pressed flat and had probably been that way for at least two decades.

She laid her purse aside and took the things from the plastic sack. Some grapes. A small carton of milk. And a box of sugary corn flakes—the only thing in the bunch that she actually wanted to eat. The rest was so she could have some semblance of a balanced meal.

Jessie handled the last item in the bag as if it were a bomb that might explode in her hands. A home pregnancy test. She eyed it and the food again. She didn't know which she dreaded more.

She read through the instructions for the test and peered at the small vial that was enclosed for a urine sample.

"You've got to be kidding," she mumbled.

It wasn't exactly the size of receptacle that would make collecting a specimen easy, but she went into the bathroom and made do. When she came back out, she slipped the vial in its little plastic stand and placed it on the scarred night table. She set the timer on her watch for ten minutes. And waited to see if a little blue circle would form in the bottom of the tube.

The first minute crawled by.

Jessie refused to think beyond this test. First, she had to get the results. She'd go from there. Go where exactly, she didn't know. She was sure there were rules to this game, but she didn't know them. Heck, she didn't even know the name of the game.

"Don't scream," the voice warned.

She didn't, because her throat snapped shut. She knew that voice, knew who it was without looking behind her. Jake McClendon.

Jessie instinctively scrambled toward her purse, but it wasn't on the table where she had left it. Frantically, she looked around. It was gone.

Dangling her purse on his finger, he stepped out from behind the closet door. In his other hand, he had her gun, the one she'd just bought the day before.

"You must have a whole arsenal of these things stashed away," he calmly remarked, making sure she saw that the gun was now unloaded.

She wished for an arsenal, though it probably wouldn't have done any good. He no doubt would have found others, as well. The man had the instincts of a cop, even if he didn't look like one. No tux today, but he wore fashionably tailored navy slacks. Expensive, certainly. And so was the shirt that was almost the same lapis blue as his eyes.

He tossed the gun and purse onto the bed and tipped his head to the vial. "If you don't mind, I'd like to see the results, too."

"Actually, I do mind."

"Tough. I'm staying."

That didn't come as a surprise to her. "How did you find me?" Even more important questions were, How much did he know? Did he know who she was? And what did he plan to do with her? He might just decide to kill her on the spot.

"When you left my hotel room without saying goodbye, I sent out my security people to follow you. I've had them watching you for the past two days, but I decided it was probably time we had a little talk."

Resources. The man had resources and money. Jessie had underestimated just how quickly he would be able to use those two things to locate her. "You didn't trip the alarm."

"No. The lipstick on the doorknob was a nice touch, though. Most people go for a strand of hair or a piece of thread. Not you. But then, from what I've learned about you, you don't do things the usual way."

Jessie put some starch in her posture. She would need all the composure she could marshal to get through this. And maybe even then, she wouldn't be able to talk him out of killing her.

"You can just get out."

"I don't think so. You started all of this when you came to me, remember?"

"A mistake. Now get out."

"Or what? You'll call the cops, huh?" He sat on the edge of the bed, the rusty springs creaking under his weight. "I think the cops are the last people you want to call. Tell me what you meant by all that junk you spouted in my hotel room. Why did you think I was trying to kill you?"

Jessie considered lying. Maybe she could convince

him she was schizophrenic or something. Instead, she decided to say nothing. She eased into the cracked vinyl padded chair across from him.

"What? Cat got your tongue?" he asked. "Or do you think I'll just go away if you don't talk to me? Think again, Jessie. A woman breaks into my hotel room, holds a gun on me and then accuses me of trying to kill her. Oh yeah, and of getting her pregnant. Hard to do, since I've never laid eyes or, for that matter, laid anything else on her."

"Then, if you know that, why don't you just leave?"

"I will when I get you to admit all of this was part of a blackmail scheme. You came to my hotel to extort money from me."

"No." She looked away, but he lunged off the bed and got right in her face.

"You thought you had everything figured out, didn't you?" His tone went from angry to abrasive. "You did your homework and found out about my Hodgkin's Disease. You learned all about Cryogen Labs. And your scheme might have worked if the vials hadn't been destroyed. That's the part you didn't know, the part you couldn't have known. Cryogen kept that under wraps to avoid negative publicity."

"Now will you get out?" she asked.

"Not yet. You had your say, and I want mine. Care to guess what I found out when I had you investigated?"

That got her complete attention. She forced her expression to stay calm. Well, she forced it as much as she could, considering that her heart was about to pound right out of her chest. "What?"

"That you're not really Jessie Briggs."

Her false composure slipped a considerable notch. She had to escape. But how? She didn't think he would let her out of his sight this time. Besides, he probably had his thugs waiting outside for her. "Just who am I, then?"

He didn't say anything for several moments. "You're nobody. You don't even exist. Don't you think that's odd? In this day and age, there are absolutely no records for a Jessie Briggs who comes even close to matching your description. No driver's license. No social security number. Nothing. And trust me, if there had been something, my people would have found it."

She didn't dare breathe easier yet. She could tell from the gleam in his eye that he had a trump card left to play—and that card might get her killed.

"Care to know what I did next?" he asked, slowly enunciating each word.

"No."

He ignored that and continued. "I had the fingerprints checked on your gun."

She slowly met his icy-blue stare. God, this couldn't be happening. How stupid could she have been to go to this man in the first place? She knew how dangerous McClendon was, knew what he was capable of doing, and yet she'd walked right into his waiting arms. She had all but pulled the trigger for him.

"And? What did you find out?" Jessie waited. Held her breath.

"They belong to a woman named Jessica Barrett. There's plenty of information on her. A rap sheet, for one thing. Shoplifting. Petty theft. Writing hot checks. She's twenty-eight. Born in Dallas. And matches your description to a tee. Her last job was as a cocktail waitress at a gentleman's club, and I use the words *gentleman* and *waitress* loosely. My security people say Ray's Cantina is nothing more than a sleazy strip joint known for its prostitutes and drug pushers."

His voice lowered to a dangerous level. "Would you like to tell me now that you're not the lying, scheming con artist that I know you are?"

Jessie tried not to look too relieved. "All right, so you've figured me out. The game is over. Now will you please leave?"

"No. Not until you tell me who put you up to this. Because I'm not buying that you did all of this on your own." He caught her by the shoulders. "Let me tell you my theory. My political opponent is a man named Abel Markham, the dirtiest SOB who ever wanted to sit in the Texas Legislature. He's the reason I'm running for office. I don't want him anywhere near the State Capitol Building, and he knows I can stop him."

"You're a real Boy Scout, aren't you, McClendon." Jessie figured she had nothing to lose now. She couldn't possibly rile him any more than he already was.

"No, I'm not. But I don't go around trying to trash other people's lives. I think Markham came up with this little scheme because of your most recent place of employment."

She fired a narrowed glance at him. "What do you mean?"

He mumbled something and shook his head. "A woman named Christy Mendoza worked at Ray's

Cantina, too, and she died at my ranch about eight months ago. It was an accident, but Markham's always tried to turn it into something else.''

Jessie couldn't believe he'd laid this in her lap. Too bad she couldn't question him about it. But it wasn't the right time. All she wanted was to get out of there.

"This kind of plan smacks of the dirty dealings that Markham's so fond of," he continued. "What did he want you to do? Go to the press with this idiotic notion that I'd gotten you pregnant?"

"Abel Markham doesn't travel in the same circles I do." But it was something to think about. Had her questions about Christy put a man like Markham on her trail?

"No, but he could have found you," Jake insisted. "He could have chosen you as the person to try to ruin me. Know what I think happened next? You went along with it, except at the last minute you got greedy and decided you could cut yourself in for some bigger bucks. So you came to me with that insemination story, hoping you could blackmail me. Because even if your story is a pack of lies, the media would have a field day with it. And it is a pack of lies, isn't it, Jessie?"

"Yes," she said softly.

"There was no kidnapping. No insemination. No plan to kill you. Just a dirty congressional candidate and a money-grubbing con artist who thought she'd found the goose that laid the golden egg." His grip tightened on her shoulders. "Am I right? Tell me I'm right!"

"You're right. Now please go. I'm leaving town and won't bother you again."

The shrill beeping pulsed through the room. Jessie gasped before she remembered what it was. The timer on her watch. She quickly pushed the small button to stop it.

"Well?" he prompted, when she didn't move. "Why don't we look at the results of the test together?"

"Why would you even care? You already know this was a con."

"Let's just call it idle curiosity." He picked up the box and quickly read through the instructions on the back. "It says if it's positive that a little blue circle will appear in the bottom of the tube." He caught her arm and pulled her out of the chair. "Let's have a look, shall we?"

Jake nudged her toward the night table. Jessie eyed the vial as if it were a deadly rattler. And she prayed. Because it was the only thing left to do. There was a chance. A slim chance.

"A real moment of reckoning, huh, sweetheart?" he asked. He snared her gaze for a long, cold moment, and together they turned and looked at the vial.

Jessie flattened her hand over her stomach and squeezed her eyes shut. There was no need to say anything because it was there. There. In the tube.

The blue ring.

A groan clawed its way past her throat. "Oh God," she mumbled. "Oh God."

Chapter Three

Jake frowned and looked at the watery blue ring that had appeared in bottom of the tube. According to the directions, that meant the test was positive. Positive, as in *the rabbit died*.

So the woman really was pregnant. He hadn't counted on that, but it meant nothing to him.

Or did it?

The baby wasn't his, that was for sure, but it didn't mean someone hadn't tried to use her to get to him. Well, maybe. Maybe this really was a scheme she'd come up with on her own. No kidnappers. No being held hostage for three months. Just her plot to get him to pay up. Or Markham's plot to ruin him.

Except, she did look surprised by that little ring. Stunned, really. And maybe just a little scared. There was something in those gray eyes of hers that made him want to comfort her.

He resisted. Of course.

It would be stupid to comfort her.

"I don't know why you look so shocked," he said, when she sank back onto the chair. "Just two days ago you broke into my suite and told me you were pregnant. Now you're acting like this is some big surprise.''

"It is." Her voice was hardly more than a whisper. "Seeing the proof. It's true. My God, it's true. There's really a baby.''

She put her arms on the table and leaned forward to cushion her face on them. She reminded Jake of a schoolgirl who was being punished. He only hoped she didn't start to cry. The tears would be fake, no doubt, but he didn't want to handle even fake crying right now.

He had to admit Jessie did seem genuinely upset, though. Maybe because he had discovered her lie. Yes, that was it. Or maybe because the pregnancy was unplanned, and that created a lot of personal problems for her. Without the blackmail money, her resources no doubt were limited, and she was probably trying to figure out a way to pay for her slip-up.

"Guess you'll have to call the father and let him know about that little blue ring," he calmly suggested.

Jessie raised her head slowly and gave him a look that could have frozen molten lava. "Don't you have somewhere else to go?"

"Not at the moment." He scraped his thumbnail over a strip of loose varnish on the nightstand. For some reason, he couldn't stop looking at the test tube. Such a little thing to deliver what was, apparently, a bombshell. He hadn't remembered his late wife, Anne, taking such a test. But of course, her pregnancy had been closely monitored by doctors right from the beginning.

For all the good it had done.

That's why this scheme bothered him so much. If Abel Markham had put this together, he certainly knew the right buttons to push. A pregnancy. A child. Nothing could have stirred up old wounds as much as this did. It had been nearly four years to the day since Anne died trying to give birth to their child. To their son. Four years of hell. Four years of blaming himself.

Yes, somebody knew exactly which buttons to push. If it wasn't Markham, then it was this woman. Either way, Jake wouldn't let them get away with it.

"Tell me about the baby's father," he insisted, forcing himself away from the memories of Anne and his son. "Was he in on this scheme, too?"

He hadn't thought the lava-freezing look could get worse, but it did. Significantly worse. She glared at him. Her jaw tightened, and her voice got louder with each word. "Yes, I think he's in on it up to his proverbial eyeballs. He's a bottom-feeding, pompous, smart-mouth jerk. My greatest wish is that at this very minute a bolt of lightning will come streaking down on him and fry him to a crispy critter."

"Careful. One might think you're talking about me."

She opened her mouth as if to add more to her name-calling litany, but then wearily shook her head. "Just go away."

"I will, after you look me in the eye and answer two questions. What's the name of the baby's father, and is Abel Markham the one who hired you?"

She slowly met his gaze again. "You don't want answers, McClendon. What you want is for me to lie. You want me to deny everything, so you can go home to your nice big ranch and put all of this behind you. Well, I can't do that."

"Because you think I'll call the cops. I won't. All I want is the truth."

"You mean the truth according to Jake Mc-Clendon."

"*The* truth. Is Markham behind this?"

"I don't know." She repeated it, but then her tone changed. No longer confrontational. No easily flung insults. Jessie stared at the floor and ran her fingers over her temple. "Maybe. Maybe that's why they said your name, so I would suspect you. I hadn't considered that until now."

He groaned. "Now we're back to kidnapping and vials?"

"Look, why don't you just go—"

"Not until you tell me who got you pregnant."

"All right, I'll tell you." Jessie grabbed his arm and shoved him into the tiny bathroom. She jabbed a finger at the filmy mirror and his reflection. "That's him. That's the father of this baby. Now I know you don't want that to be true. Believe me, neither do I, but I can't change things. I can't go back three months and stop myself from being kidnapped. I can't stop them from violating me and using me as some pawn in their sick game."

The burst of emotion left as quickly as it came. She sagged against the wall. "Will you please just go?"

"Not yet." He roughly cupped her chin, forcing her to look at him. "Give me one good reason why I should believe anything you've said. I know who you are, remember? I know you worked at some sleazy joint where you probably turned tricks on the side or danced naked on tables for money.''

Her mouth dropped open. ''I was a cocktail waitress. Look at me, for heaven's sake. Do I look like a hooker or exotic dancer?'' Jake did look at her. She was still sickly pale, and it seemed as if she'd cut her hair with a dull weed whacker. Far from sexy. Still, there was something appealing about her. The mouth, he figured. It was full and sensuous. That mouth would attract some men. And her eyes. When she wasn't ready to spit bullets at him, her eyes mellowed to a soft platinum color.

His gaze traveled downward. Voluptuous, she wasn't. Not by anybody's standards. Her breasts were small, well-shaped, and because she obviously wasn't wearing a bra, he could see her nipples pressed against the stretchy fabric of her top. After feeling his body clench, he decided it wasn't good to look at her breasts. Jessie Barrett might be a natural-born liar, and pregnant, but for reasons he didn't want to explore, his body seemed to respond to her.

Her waist was small, as well. A flat stomach that made him wonder just how many weeks' pregnant she really was. The jeans she wore gapped at the waist and barely skimmed over her hips. Her legs, like the rest of her, were slender. And long. She was easily five feet eight inches tall. He was just over six feet and didn't have to drop his gaze too much to look her in the eye.

Not that he especially wanted to look into her eyes.

''Well?'' she demanded.

Jake realized she was still waiting for an answer. Somehow, he'd forgotten the question. ''Well what?''

She pushed out a frustrated breath. "Do I look like I could earn a living with this body?"

Maybe not earn a living, but she could do a fair job of stirring him up. Best to keep that to himself. It'd been a long time since he'd felt a physical attraction for a woman. Any woman. He wasn't about to let his libido *stir* him in her direction.

She shook her head. "Don't bother answering. I know what I look like, especially now. Trust me, you wouldn't look much better if you'd been through what I have." She gave a tired, cynical laugh. "You actually thought I was a hooker. What a joke. I don't even like sex, and I haven't been with a man in years."

It didn't seem a subject he wanted to explore. With her, anyway. He liked sex. And missed having it. She reminded him of that.

"Besides," she continued, "my job and lifestyle have nothing to do with what went on at that warehouse."

Maybe. But he wasn't about to discount it yet. "So you're sticking to the story that this kidnapping really happened?"

She squeezed her hands into fists, groaned in frustration and stormed out of the room. Jake followed her because he didn't want her to try to escape again. He was still looking for answers, and she was his best bet. Maybe his only bet.

He caught her wrist and whirled her around to face him. Not the best idea he'd ever had. It caused a major problem. Because of the way he turned her, Jessie really faced him. Right up close. Barely inches away. And her warm, rapid breath hit against his throat.

Jake took in her scent, then. Not the smell of the cheap motel room, or even odors from the sweltering Texas heat outside. *Her* scent. A mingle of everything that was female. And something else. Something deeper, that he thought he might recognize but didn't want to.

Great. He was obviously letting this fast-breathing, skinny liar get to him. He couldn't possibly recognize her scent because there was nothing about it to recognize. Nothing. He didn't know her, and she only knew him in the confines of her warped imagination.

Still, he felt the uncomfortable shiver go down his spine. It seemed a primitive signal that tried to override his common sense. Well, Jake had news for primitive signals—nothing overrode his common sense.

Nothing.

''How long are you going to hang around here and harass me?'' Jessie demanded. She looked resolute enough. Her back was stiff, her chin up. Her eyes were focused and narrowed. But then he heard her swallow. She gulped. As if all of this closeness had some kind of weird effect on her, too.

Jake shook his head to clear it. If there was some kind of odd feeling between them, he didn't want to explore it. Not with this woman. ''I'll hang around and harass you, as you call it, until I get the truth.''

''I've told you the truth, but you've chosen not to believe it. Well, you know what? That's fine, as long as you get out of here and leave me alone. I think I'd like to have a nervous breakdown now and I can't do that with you calling me a liar every few minutes.''

"Your nervous breakdown will have to wait."
Jake glanced at the blue circle in the vial again, and
then at her. He had some things to work out and there
was only one place to start. With her. "Come on. I
think I know of a way we can settle all of this right
now." He caught her by the arm, but she shook off
his grip just as quickly.

"What do you mean by *come on?* Do you honestly
think I'd go anywhere with you?"

"I don't think you have a choice. I can still call
the cops, remember?"

She threw up her hands. "Then, why don't you?
Go ahead. I want you to do it. Since I don't have a
phone, that means you'll have to go elsewhere to
make that call, and elsewhere is exactly where I want
you to be."

"I will be elsewhere. Soon. All I want is to get
some facts straight, and we can do that with a visit
to Cryogen Labs. If I remember correctly, it's open
until eight. We'll have plenty of time to get there
before they close."

"And just what would that accomplish?"

"They can tell you to your lying face that my vials
were destroyed four months ago."

Again, she gave him one of those gritty looks.
"And? Why would I believe them, when I saw proof
that one existed?"

Jake tried to put a choke hold on what was left of
his self-control. Somehow, he had to get her to confess that she'd lied, and yelling at her didn't seem to
work. Nor did intimidation. Actually, so far nothing
had worked.

"Look, this visit isn't just for me," he explained,

forcing himself to calm down. "It could give you some peace of mind, too."

Her hands went to her hips. "How, pray tell?"

"If you really believe this asinine theory of kidnapping and insemination, then it stands to reason that someone at Cryogen was in on this. Only a handful of people work there. You could see if you recognize them."

"I didn't see their faces. They wore surgical masks."

Of course. What else had he expected her to say? "Maybe you could recognize their voices?"

She rearranged her expression, apparently giving that some thought. "Maybe." But then she shook her head. "I can't go walking into Cryogen Labs. Someone wants to kill me, remember? It could be the people who work there."

"Oh, yes. That." He didn't intend to let her get away that easily, not when he was this close to the truth. "Well, I can't imagine anyone trying to kill you with a witness around, and I make one heck of a witness. Don't worry. Nothing bad will happen while you're with me."

JESSIE DIDN'T HAVE a good feeling about this little trip at all, and Jake McClendon's assurance was probably worth a thimble full of spit. *Nothing bad will happen while you're with me.*

Yeah, right.

Easy for him to say. Nobody wanted to kill him. Well, except for her. And that was only in a figurative sense.

"You're not about to throw up, are you?" he asked.

It was the first thing Jake had said since he forced her into his sleek silver luxury car. This was probably his idea of chitchat. Fine. Her idea of answering him was to continue to look out the window as he drove down St. Mary's Street.

"Because you look like you're about to throw up," he added.

This wasn't a conversation Jessie wanted to have. Her stomach was queasy enough as it was, without discussing the potential outcome of queasiness. "Will you leave me alone? If and when I have to throw up, you'll be the first to know. Well, maybe the second. What? Are you afraid I'll ruin the carpet in your overpriced, foreign car?"

"No. I'm more concerned about that look on your face. When's the last time you had something to eat?"

It took Jessie several moments to gather her breath so she could answer him. "I'm not sure."

"Well, I'm getting some food in you."

She frowned at the concern she saw when she glanced at him. "What's with you? One minute you threaten to call the cops, and the next minute you want to feed me? Make up your mind, McClendon. All this flip-flopping is making me dizzy."

"Feeding you has nothing to do with whether or not I believe you're a con artist. Right now, I'm thinking about that baby you're carrying."

Jessie felt as if he'd punched her. She didn't want him to think about the baby. Well, not beyond thinking about how it fit into the general scheme of things, she didn't. She certainly didn't want him concerned about it.

"What I had in mind was going through a drive-thru to get you a soft drink or something," he added. "It might settle your stomach."

"I'm fine. Don't worry about me or my stomach."

"I wasn't worrying." But he turned into the parking lot of a fast-food place and stopped in front of the huge menu board. "What do you want to eat?"

She fired him an annoyed glance. "Nothing."

"If you don't tell me, I'll just order for you."

The cheerful, young voice on the speaker welcomed them and asked what she could do for them. Jessie ignored the voice. "Are you always this pushy, Mr. McClendon?"

"Always."

She didn't doubt him. And she didn't want to argue. Besides, some food just might help her queasy stomach. "A cheeseburger and a chocolate milk shake." She reached into her pocket, pulled out a five-dollar bill and tossed it into his lap.

"I'll pay for it." And he picked up the money and sent it right back in her direction.

"No. You won't." She wouldn't budge on this, either. She didn't want one cent of his money.

Jessie latched on to the bill just as he latched on to her hand. She supposed he was trying to stuff the money back into her pocket. He succeeded.

Well, to some extent.

He got his fingers, and the five, about halfway into the front pocket of her jeans before it must have occurred to him that wasn't a place his hand should be. It also occurred to Jessie that having his hand there felt somewhat better than it should have. He managed to touch some kind of nerve that went from her hipbone all the way to a place that suddenly seemed filled with nerves.

Jake snatched back his hand, leaving the money sticking out of her pocket. The cheerful voice on the speaker asked them if they needed more time to make up their minds about the order. Neither answered her.

Jessie glanced at the five. Then at him. "This money is going somewhere on your body, preferably your shirt pocket. But don't tempt me."

When he didn't take it, she slipped the bill into his pocket, trying to touch as little of him as possible. It was hard not to notice that solid chest, though. Very solid. Lord, she hoped that wasn't his nipple her fingers grazed. Judging from the way he sucked in his breath, it was.

Scowling, Jake ordered for her and added a hamburger combo meal for himself. After he paid for the food and picked it up at the window, he parked in a spot near the street. That made Jessie feel a little better. If necessary, they could make a quick getaway. Well, maybe. Since her host didn't believe her, he might not realize in time that there was anything to get away from.

"So who are you, really?" he asked.

She shoved the plastic straw into her drink and took a sip, before placing the milk shake in the cup holder. "We've been through that, and I'm not up to another argument. If you want conversation with your burger, then pick a less volatile subject."

"All right." His hesitation let her know he couldn't come up with anything right away. "Why did you become a cocktail waitress?"

"What you really mean is, why didn't I become something better?"

"If that's what I wanted to know, I would have

asked. I don't mince words, and I'm trying not to be *volatile* here.''

Jessie nibbled on her cheeseburger so it would give her time to think up an answer. ''I only worked at the cantina for a week, but I suppose I became a waitress because I like the idea of eating regularly and paying my bills. That's something I'm sure you've never had to worry about.''

There was no stinging comeback. No sarcasm. Just silence. Jessie glanced at him to make sure he wasn't quietly choking on his burger. He wasn't. He was staring at her.

The light came through the window at an odd angle, slanting over his face. A strong face. Handsome, she reluctantly admitted.

Yes.

There it was again. That odd feeling when she looked at him. More than a twinge. Less than a jolt. Something. Something, she didn't want to feel. What the heck was it about this overbearing man that made her insides turn to mush?

''What?'' he asked.

''What do you mean *what?*''

''You're looking at me.''

Well, he started it. Jessie forced her gaze away. ''Sorry. I didn't know looking at someone was against the law.''

''It isn't. Under normal circumstances,'' he mumbled, making it sound like an afterthought. ''Listen, let's declare a short truce. That way, you can do more than pick at that cheeseburger, and neither of us will get indigestion.''

It was too late. She already had indigestion. Jessie reached for her milk shake just as he reached for his drink. The back of his hand grazed hers. It was only a whisper of a touch. She might not have noticed it if it had been another man. This time she noticed. Apparently so did he, because when she glanced up, he had his gaze fixed on her.

Mush again.

She looked at his mouth. It was a well-shaped mouth. He was probably a champion kisser. Now why the heck had she thought of something like that? To the best of her knowledge, she'd never, never looked at a man and declared him a champion kisser.

Along with the indigestion, she was probably losing it.

This was stupid. Just plain stupid. She didn't get all hot and bothered when she looked at a man's mouth. Especially the mouth of a man she didn't trust.

"Go ahead," Jessie mumbled. "Say something volatile."

His hamburger stopped halfway to his mouth. "Huh?"

Jessie couldn't tell him she needed an attitude adjustment, but she did. If he said something irritating, it would probably get her back on track. It would at least get her attention off his mouth.

"Volatile," she repeated. "Ask me more of those dumb questions. Accuse me of being a hooker or a stripper. Anything."

He frowned. "Are you having that nervous breakdown now?"

No, but it might be a good time for it. "We should go," she said quickly. "I don't want to waste any more time sitting around here."

He mumbled something under his breath and

shoved his burger back into the paper sack. He had the car started and back on the street within seconds.

From the corner of her eye, she saw his grip tighten on the steering wheel. "I'm surprised you haven't tried to jump out of the car by now," he commented.

Now he came up with the volatile stuff. A bit late but still effective. It got her mind off him and onto her situation.

Jessie had considered jumping out of the car, but had ruled it out. She really didn't want a bunch of scrapes and bruises, especially when he no doubt had someone following them. If she did try to jump out, then one of his hired goons would likely grab her and put her back into the car. Besides, this trip to Cryogen Labs just might provide her with some answers.

"I guess I'm just not in the mood for jumping out of cars," she said. She put the rest of her cheeseburger into the bag and leaned her head against the back of the seat.

"So what are you in the mood for—talking?"

"Not that, either. I'll be in the mood for talking when you're in the mood to listen."

He mumbled under his breath again. "You might have to wait a couple hundred years for that. Well, unless you're interested in telling me the truth."

"I've already told you the truth." Well, as much of the truth as she knew.

Just what was the whole truth, anyway?

Had this man, Abel Markham, used her as his pawn? Or was Jake McClendon the mastermind? Maybe it was neither of them. Maybe it was someone she hadn't even considered. If that was true, then she was back to square one, the same place she'd been for days.

"Well, there's your Waterloo," he said, pointing to the building that lay ahead. "Cryogen Labs. Are you sure you don't want to come clean now? It could save you from being humiliated."

"The only person risking humiliation is you." But Jessie had no idea if that was even true.

Cryogen Labs looked innocuous enough with its buttermilk-colored brick exterior and white lacquered shutters, but it still frightened her enough to make her tremble. With reason. Somehow, somebody connected with that lab had possibly been in on the plan to kidnap her. The plan that had resulted in her becoming pregnant.

Pregnant.

She gulped in a deep breath and tried to shake off that thought. It wasn't the time to think about the ramifications of a pregnancy. Or the baby. It would only distract her. She couldn't afford any more distractions now. Later, she would work out what she was going to do.

Jake parked his car, and they walked toward the building. "Well, I have to give it to you, Ms. Barrett. I really thought you'd try to run away by now."

She came to a complete stop and spun around, intending to give him a piece of her mind. The only thing she gave him was a weak head butt to his shoulder, when the dizzy spell sent her right into him. Her legs turned to rubber, and he caught her in his arms.

"Christ," he mumbled. "Are you all right?"

Jessie tried to nod and push herself away from him. She failed. Because it seemed she had no other choice, she rested her head against his shoulder and tried to wait out the dizziness.

He smelled good. Warm and musky. There was the underlying scent of an expensive aftershave. And his arm that slid around her waist was strong, corded with muscles. The smooth fabric of his shirt sleeve brushed against her arm. Sweet heaven. She didn't want this. Too bad her head was in the middle of her own personal F-5 tornado.

"Take a deep breath," he instructed.

She did. It helped a little. "I hate this light-headedness."

"I can see why. It's hard to work out diabolical schemes when you're as pale as a ghost and ready to lose your lunch."

Jessie forced her eyes to focus. She didn't think she quite managed a scowl, but she tried. Especially when she realized how close they were. Her body was pressed against his. Right against his. Even through her cotton shirt, she could feel his belt buckle on her stomach. She wouldn't think about anything below his belt, even though she would have had to be paralyzed not to notice he was a man. All man.

Their faces were so close she could count his eyelashes, which were too long, she decided. His breath was sweet. From the soft drink, not his disposition. He also needed a shave. His five o'clock shadow was dark and coarse. And it made him look a little like an outlaw. She wouldn't allow herself to look at his mouth. No. Even the dizziness wouldn't counteract that. That mouth had her hormonal number.

She stepped back. "Thank you, Mr. McClendon,

for reminding me that you're a jerk. No, worse than a jerk. You're navel lint.''

"Anytime." But his comment lacked sarcasm.

When Jessie glanced up, she saw more of that concern in his expression. He was still close, despite that step she had taken away from him. She took another, but he caught her arm. She was thankful. The inside of her head was still whirling around. If he hadn't caught her, she no doubt would have fallen on her face.

"Let's go in," she insisted. "That way, I can sit down, and you don't have to hold me.''

"Don't worry. I'm not holding you for your sake. My concern is for your child. I don't want you blaming me for pushing you too hard."

She gave a hollow laugh. "That's a joke, right? You've done nothing but push me hard. You've hounded me, harassed me and called me names."

He didn't say anything for several seconds. "I want answers, and I'm sorry if you don't like my methods. Once we're through inside, your game will be over. You can get out of my face and I can get out of yours."

"Good." She wiggled out of his grip and walked to the door on her own. Fortunately, the anger eased the dizziness.

"Yes. Good." He jerked open the door and led her inside.

The reception area looked like any other place of business. Monochrome shades of beige. It looked too clean. Almost sterile, which seemed ironic to Jessie, since the place stored one of the most basic elements needed for human reproduction.

The blond woman behind the desk greeted them

with a businesslike smile. "Welcome to Cryogen Labs. How may I help you?"

"I'm Jake McClendon."

"Yes, Mr. McClendon." The perky-looking blonde became flustered and blushed. "Wow, it really is you. I saw you on the news, but you look much better in person."

Jessie tried not to roll her eyes. The icing on the cake. A fan of Jake McClendon's. It was bad enough that she had to be here with him, but now she had to experience some woman who was neck-deep in hero worship, as well. That sexy mouth of his must have the same effect on all females.

Apparently he didn't want to indulge too much in the adoration, either, because he got right to the point. "I need to speak to Dr. Radelman."

"Oh. He doesn't work here anymore."

"Since when? He's the man who contacted me after my vials were destroyed."

"Yes, and he left, um, let me see when..." She flipped through her calendar. "About two weeks later."

Two weeks after the vials were destroyed and about two weeks before someone kidnapped her. Jessie didn't think that was a coincidence. A doctor probably would have been the one to do the actual insemination.

"Why did Dr. Radelman leave?" Jake demanded.

"He transferred to another job." She snapped her fingers as if trying to recall something. "Harvest Place, I think it's called. Something like that, anyway. It's not connected with Cryogen."

Jessie started to ask if the woman had the address or phone number of the place, but Jake spoke before she could. "There was a nurse who worked here. She had a soft voice and she was tall. Red hair. She wasn't the one I spoke to on the phone a couple of days ago."

Soft voice. That got Jessie's attention. The woman who held her captive had had a soft voice. And she'd no doubt been a nurse, since she was the one who had administered the injections. She was tall, too. Jessie remembered that about her, even though she'd never seen the woman's face. Nor her hair. Her hair had always been bundled under a surgical cap. But the eyes. Yes, she'd seen her eyes. And they were dark green.

"You must mean Marion Cameron," the blonde said with a grin. "But she doesn't work here anymore, either. She left the same time Dr. Radelman did."

Jake shook his head in apparent frustration. "To take another job?"

The woman shrugged. "A sabbatical. She'd been under a lot of stress. Her husband walked out on her, so she was going through all this emotional stuff."

"Does she have green eyes?" Jessie asked.

Jake looked at her.

So did the blonde, who said, "Yes, as a matter of fact she does."

Jessie didn't know whether to be relieved or not. Finally, there was some proof, little though it was, to back up what she'd been saying.

"Thank you for the information," Jake told the woman. "By any chance do you have addresses for Marion Cameron and Dr. Radelman?"

"Sorry." The blush on her cheeks deepened. "I'm not allowed to give that out."

Jessie thought he might argue, but he didn't. That was probably because he knew his people could easily come up with that kind of information. He took her by the arm and led her out of the building.

"Still think I'm lying?" she asked briskly, as they walked across the parking lot.

He didn't answer for several seconds. "Yes."

Of course. What had she expected? "But what about the missing doctor and nurse? You can't believe it's a coincidence they would leave right after your vials were supposedly destroyed."

"I don't know what to believe yet—not until I've spoken with them." He put his hand on the car door, but didn't open it. "I'll make some calls and find out where they are."

"And then what?"

His mouth thinned. "Well, I won't be buying cigars anytime soon. Even if by some miracle these people were involved in a plot to kidnap you, it doesn't mean you're carrying my baby."

Jessie would have returned verbal fire, but she caught some movement out of the corner of her eye. A late-model, white, four-door sedan. And it was going much too slowly. She turned toward it, her own body seemingly moving in slow motion, as well. Before she could respond, before she could brace herself, there was a deafening blast. The back window of Jake's car shattered and the pebbled sheet of safety glass crashed onto the seat with a walloping *thud*.

"Get down!" she yelled. Jake shouted something similar at the same time, but he punctuated it with some vicious profanity.

A rapid fire of bullets sizzled across the roof. Just like that, in the span of a heartbeat, Jessie's anger evaporated. In its place, her instincts kicked in. And her fear. A sickening fear that clawed away at her. God, she didn't want to die this way.

She hit the pavement, her knees catching the brunt of the fall. Jake shoved her the rest of the way down and followed on top of her, sheltering her body with his. She got only a glimpse of a man in the white car.

"Someone's shooting at us." But it wasn't necessary for Jessie to relay that information. Jake apparently knew exactly what was happening.

It was an awful time to say that she told him so, but blast it, she had told him so. *Nothing bad will happen while you're with me.* Yeah, right. She'd warned him that somebody wanted her dead and he hadn't believed her. Well, maybe this would finally convince him.

If they lived long enough for it to convince him.

A bullet, then another, tore into the car. The sounds of lead ripping through metal were all around them. Her heart was in her throat. And her pulse pounded violently. Her every instinct screamed for her to fight back. To protect herself. But there was no way to do that in an open parking lot.

A thousand thoughts crossed her mind. None good. This was the culmination of her worst fears. She was unarmed, with a gunman after her. This time, he just might succeed in killing her. Maybe even killing Jake, as well. They could both die right here, right now, and she wouldn't even know why she'd been murdered.

There was the squeal of tires, followed by another shot. She didn't dare hope the gunman was leaving. From the sound of it, he was simply circling around to get a better angle. Jessie sucked in a hard breath, trying to keep the veneer over the panic that was so close to the surface she could taste it, fiery and bitter in her mouth.

Jake pressed himself against her, a reminder that he had placed himself right in the path of those bullets. Like hers, his breath came out in short, fast spurts. Jessie could feel the knots in his muscles. The hot scent of adrenaline and scorched metal was all around them.

When the white car momentarily darted out of her line of sight, Jake reached up and fumbled around until he located the handle. He popped open the door. "Stay down and get on the floor."

He rolled to his side so she could slip into the car. Doing so, he put himself in even greater danger. Jessie wouldn't let herself consider why he did that. No use thinking about him as a Boy Scout.

She crunched herself as far under the dash as she could and latched onto his shirt. "Get in!" she yelled.

He did. Somehow, he snaked through the narrow opening and across the seats, slamming the door behind him. Within seconds he had the car started and gunned the engine.

They sped away, just as another bullet demolished the window right above Jessie's head.

Chapter Four

"Are you hit?" Jake yelled as he maneuvered his car through a hairpin turn.

Jessie did a quick inventory. "No. You?"

"No, but stay down."

"I could say the same to you." But he didn't stay down. He continued to speed away from the person who had just tried to kill them. Or her. Jessie suspected those bullets had been meant for her.

God, would this nightmare ever end?

"Is he following us?" she asked, unable to see for herself. But she didn't have to wait for Jake to answer. Another bullet skipped off the roof, gashing into the metal and even the leather interior just overhead. Someone meant business. "Did you get a look at the gunman?"

"Just a man in a white car. The first digit of the license plate was *C*."

"The last was *F*," Jessie provided, after she pulled in a generous breath. Not that it helped. Every inch of her was on a razor-sharp edge, her body braced for the fight. A fight she could easily lose. And losing this fight would mean dying. "There was mud or something covering the rest of the plate. I think it might be the same man who kidnapped me.''

Jake made another turn, his gaze darting between the rearview mirror and the street ahead. ''I thought you said there were four people who kidnapped you.''

''There were. Three men and a woman, for sure. My guess is one of the men was Dr. Radelman. The woman could have been Marion Cameron. That leaves the two goons who tied me up and dumped me in the back of a van. Anytime they needed muscle, they brought in one of them.''

Jake didn't say anything for a while. ''Well, whoever our shooter is, he's apparently decided not to come after us. He turned on that last street.''

That didn't make her relax one bit. It only meant the gunman wouldn't pursue them now. It didn't mean she was safe. For that matter, apparently neither was Jake. The shooter hadn't even tried to keep those bullets aimed specifically at her. And that troubled Jessie. A lot. A hired killer probably wouldn't have risked killing his boss. So just who was this man who'd fired these shots? She hoped she didn't have to wait long to find out.

''Don't get up yet,'' Jake insisted, when she started to move.

Jessie didn't like taking orders from him. After all, he was the one who had put them in danger by insisting they go to Cryogen Labs. But if they hadn't gone, she might not have learned the names of two of the people who were likely involved in her kidnapping.

Now all they had to do was find those people and get them to confess. She wouldn't hold her breath waiting for that to happen, but now that she had names, maybe she could get Byron to check them out. Of course, involving Byron any further probably wasn't a smart idea. His job would be on the line if anyone found out how he'd already helped her.

Jake pulled the phone from the console and began to press in some numbers.

"Who are you calling?" she asked, returning to the seat.

"Who do you think? The cops."

Jessie desperately wanted to stop him, but she couldn't think of a reason to give him. Besides, it was logical to bring in the police. Someone had tried to kill them. Still... "How much will you tell them?"

He stopped the call and gave her a considering glance. "What do you mean? I'll tell them the truth."

"All of it, even the parts about me?"

Jake paused. Frowned. "You know, that's something else that bothers me about you. Why haven't you gone to the cops already? If you had, maybe this shooting wouldn't have happened."

She should have anticipated his question. It was logical. Too bad she didn't have a logical explanation she could give him. "I have my reasons for trying to work this out myself."

"And what would those reasons be?" he asked sarcastically.

"My own business."

"Wrong answer. When people start shooting at me to get to you, it's *my* business. Now why didn't you go to the cops when you supposedly escaped from these kidnappers?"

She stared at him for a moment, shook her head and glanced away. "Because I thought I could handle this. I figured the minute the cops were called in, then these people would cover their tracks so fast I'd never find them."

"And?" he prompted. "There's more to it than that. You knew you shouldn't be investigating something like this. Besides, as far as I can tell, you were hiding out, not investigating."

Not true. That trip to his hotel room had been a fact-finding mission. Too bad it had been a dumb idea. It had also been dumb to involve Byron in all of this. Some friend she was—it could cost him everything. Still, if Jessie thought the police could help, she would have called them despite the consequences.

"If I went to the cops and told them I suspected you of kidnapping me, who do you think they would believe? Certainly not me."

"Ah. You mean because of your criminal record? Well, you'll just have to put aside your distrust of law enforcement and let them do their job. You don't have a choice."

Apparently, he was right. Especially since she didn't know what else to do. Jessie didn't say another word, while he made the call. She sat quietly and listened as he related the shooting incident. And as he identified her as his *passenger*. What he didn't mention was the kidnapping or the other things she'd told him. He would. She was sure of it.

Jessie glanced out the window. Her hands still trembled from the shooting, so she clenched them together. If she somehow managed to get out of the car before it arrived at the station, Jake would still probably give the cops a detailed account of everything she'd told him. Worse, he would no doubt implicate her in the insemination plot. Then, the police would be searching for her.

That would eventually lead them to Byron.

On the other hand, she didn't think she could talk Jake into keeping her secrets. No, he would tell, all right. Men like him reported crimes. And she'd have to verify it. Jessie couldn't see a way around that. But she wouldn't have to let the cops in on everything—only what she'd told Jake. Only what she wanted him to know for the time being. She could protect Byron a little longer, until she figured out what to do.

"I'm sorry," he said after a while. "I shouldn't have brought you to Cryogen Labs with me."

Jessie glanced over at him, but he looked straight ahead, focused on the street. "Is that like an apology?"

He scowled, bunching up his forehead. "Yes, I suppose it is. Until we get all of this figured out, I want to offer you protection. A bodyguard, maybe. It doesn't mean I believe everything you've told me, but I can see now that you're in danger."

Jessie started to give him a snippy comeback, but her heart wasn't in it. She was too exhausted to go another round with him. "I don't need your bodyguard."

"No, but your baby does. Have you thought about that?"

She hadn't. And Jessie didn't want to think about it, either. Not now. So far, in her mind, the baby was just a vague notion along with a little blue circle in the bottom of a test tube. She wanted to keep it that way for a while.

"We'll call this my good deed for the day," Jake continued.

That didn't sit well with her at all. "And this is coming from the man who said nothing bad would happen while I'm with you. How many rounds do you think that gunman fired at us?"

"Listen, you're the one who dragged me into this." He shoved a thumb against his chest. "You came to me, remember? Now I intend to finish it, and I'll do that by providing you protection whether you want it or not. Got that?"

Yes, she *got that.* She only hoped it didn't cost both of them their lives. Or worse. Jake was right about one thing. Little blue circles in test tubes didn't need protection. But babies did.

Yes, babies did.

Now, she had another life to worry about. If she couldn't protect herself, she couldn't protect the baby.

Her baby.

And protecting the baby suddenly seemed the most important thing in the world.

IT WAS DARK by the time they finished at the police station, even though they had their statements taken almost immediately. The cops also agreed not to release information about Jessie. They wanted time to check out her story and see what they could find out about Dr. Radelman and Marion Cameron.

For the most part Jessie had cooperated with the officers, but Jake noticed that she looked uncomfortable. That was natural, he supposed. Other than a couple of barroom fights, he'd had no run-ins with the law, but Jessie couldn't say the same. With her priors, she probably felt like a frequent sinner standing at the Pearly Gates.

While Jessie gave her statement, Jake called his housekeeper at the ranch to let her know they'd be arriving. He also had one of the ranch hands drop him off another car, since the cops wanted to keep his to recover any bullet fragments.

"Where do you think you're taking me now?" Jessie asked, when they left the station. She glanced at the grip he had on her arm and pushed his hand away.

"To my ranch. It's north of San Antonio. You'll be safe there."

She didn't argue. Probably because she was worn-out. He remembered Anne being tired early in her pregnancy and guessed that Jessie was going through the same thing. With reason. She wasn't just experiencing the symptoms of pregnancy; it seemed there was someone who wanted her dead.

He started the half-hour drive to his Hill Country ranch. Somewhere along the way, Jessie fell asleep. He wouldn't have known if he hadn't actually looked at her. There was no noticeable change in her breathing pattern—she merely leaned her head against the window and slept. Jake was thankful for it because it gave him some time to try to figure out the next step.

He could just turn the whole matter over to the police. Maybe they would even provide Jessie with adequate protection. That way, if this was some kind of plot to ruin him politically, then the investigation would be official and aboveboard. Hopefully, the cops would look at Abel Markham first.

There was just one problem with that plan—Markham might get to Jessie before the police could gather enough evidence on him. He might even kill her.

"Hell," he mumbled under his breath. The woman might be a smart-mouthed pain in the butt, but he didn't want her dead. Especially if she was a pawn in Markham's plot.

There was also the baby to consider. He just didn't know what to do about it, and it was best that he kept it that way. Jake didn't even want to think about the possibility that she'd told him the truth about the baby. He'd just be setting himself up for more pain. No, the child wasn't his.

It couldn't be his.

He glanced at Jessie again. Even in sleep she wasn't resting. The muscles in her face were tense. Her fists were clenched. She had her teeth clamped over her bottom lip, as if afraid she might say something she shouldn't. What kind of demons did she wrestle now? He knew a lot about demons, had wrestled them for years. And he recognized all the signs.

Jake used the remote to open the security gates that fronted his property, and drove inside. The trio of Dobermans shot out from the darkness and began to bark. The sound must have jarred Jessie because her eyelids flew open.

She jerked toward him. "What's wrong?"

"Nothing. It's just the guard dogs. They'll stop when they realize it's me." And they did a moment later, even though they continued to race alongside the car.

Jessie rubbed her eyes and looked out the window at the ranch. "This is some place you've got here."

Sprawling was the word most people used to describe it, and it was. He owned about two thousand acres, and the main house was right in the middle of it.

When his mother had designed the place nearly twenty years earlier, she'd said she wanted *space*. Jake figured there was about ten thousand square feet of it inside the three stories of natural white limestone and ponderosa pine. It had always reminded him of an intricate tree house with decks and balconies. Still, it fit perfectly in the Hill Country setting. And it fit him perfectly.

He got out, sent the dogs on their way and opened the door for Jessie. "Would you like for me to carry you in?"

She gave him another of those flinty looks. "No, thanks. If I go anywhere, I'll walk."

And she did, even though Jake noticed she gripped on to the railing when they went up the steps to the house. "You have a security system?" she asked.

"State of the art. The grounds are rigged with surveillance detectors and the dogs are out at all times."

"Pretty serious equipment for a cattle ranch."

She made the remark sound off-the-cuff, but Jake knew she had to be concerned about her safety. "We had a problem here late last year, so I upgraded the whole security system."

Jessie paused on the top step and looked back at him. "You mean the death of that woman who worked at Ray's Cantina?"

"Yes. She was part of the catering staff I'd hired for a party. Did you know her?"

Even in the darkness, he saw something flicker in her eyes. A look of tired sadness. But she quickly glanced away.

"Not really," she finally answered. "She died before I started to work for Ray."

But she'd obviously heard some things. Gossip that no doubt implicated him. "The woman wandered away from the house and accidentally drowned in the pond," he explained, wondering why he felt he owed her any explanation. "After that, I decided I didn't want anyone to take impromptu walks around the place unless I knew about it."

Jessie didn't utter a word. She simply stared into the darkness. But he heard the shudder of her breath.

Jake caught on to her arm again. "Come on. Let's get inside."

As he expected, his housekeeper, Ellen, met them at the door, and he introduced the women to each other. "Ellen will fix you something hot to eat and then show you to your room."

"Thank you," Jessie answered softly.

Again, he noticed how pale she was and wondered if he should call the doctor. If she didn't look better by morning, he would. "I have some calls to make and then I'll try to get some sleep. You do the same, okay?"

She gave him a weak nod and followed his housekeeper out of the room. Jake stood there for a minute, his gaze still on the spot Jessie had just occupied.

He cursed himself for being so concerned about her. He didn't need to make any kind of emotional investment in a woman who was bound to be nothing but trouble.

The sooner he got her out of his life, the better.

SOMETHING WOKE HER UP in the night. A soft *swish*. On a ragged gasp, Jessie snapped to a sitting position and listened to make sure someone hadn't broken in. She looked around the unfamiliar bedroom, got her bearings and took a deep breath of relief. She was alone.

No one had come for her tonight.

There would be no scuffle. No one to grab her and shove a chloroform-soaked rag against her face. No warehouse. No kidnappers. Tonight, there was just the sickening memories and the uncertainty to disturb her.

She glanced at the clock. It was two in the morning. Outside, the wind kicked up as if a storm was on the way. Tossing back the covers, she got up, walked to the balcony doors and looked outside. No storm. Just a clear sky, speckled with stars and a thumbnail moon. The view was breathtaking.

She eased open the doors and stepped onto the balcony. The wood was cool beneath her bare feet. Jessie pushed her hair away from her face and let the breeze wash over her.

The scent of the cedars and mesquites was all around, but she also thought she detected the faint smell of smoke. And maybe whiskey. Since she didn't see any indication of a fire on the grounds, she figured that someone had burned brush earlier and the wind had blown it in the direction of the house.

Jessie prayed that was all there was to it, anyway.

From the corner of her eye, she caught some slight motion, a small flicker of light. She reeled toward it, reaching for a gun that wasn't there. But a gun wasn't necessary. At least, she didn't think it was. It was Jake. Jake, watching her. He was smoking a thin brown cigar.

He stood on the other side of the balcony, facing her, only five yards or so of empty space between them. His bare feet were crossed at the ankles. He had his back casually propped against the thick pine railing. And he was naked.

Jessie blinked and looked at him again. Not quite naked. But he wore only a pair of tan-colored boxer shorts. The breeze molded them to his body, revealing everything the fabric covered.

He calmly crushed out the cigar in the empty shot glass he held. "Is there something I can do for you, Jessie?"

As questions went, it was the most leading one she'd ever been asked. She forced herself to remember that she really didn't trust him. Hard to do, considering her body went all warm and golden when she looked at him.

Physically he was, well, close to perfect, from his chiseled chest sprinkled with hair to his washboard stomach. And his body was something she shouldn't gawk at.

"You smoke?" she asked.

She winced at the trivial question. Now that was true genius coming up with that. Why hadn't she just said a hasty good-night and gone back in? She didn't need to be out there. She didn't need to be within a mile of him while he was undressed like that.

"Not really," he answered.

Confused, she tipped her head to the cigar butt in the shot glass. "But you just finished one."

He shrugged. "I needed something to calm my nerves, I guess."

It'd worked. He looked calm. Well, except for that one tight muscle that ran the length of his jaw. And maybe his eyes were narrowed just slightly.

Jessie looked closely. She didn't want to notice it, but he was aroused. Hard not to notice that. She'd obviously interrupted some very private…thoughts.

Mercy.

Why should his arousal make her feel anything, especially hot and tingly? She reminded her body that it was preparing itself for something it wouldn't get. Jake and his arousal were not options, no matter how hot and tingly she got.

Frustrated with herself and her reaction, she fluttered her fingers toward her room. ''I should go back in. Good night.''

Jessie didn't wait for him to answer. She turned and caught her reflection in the glass. And her mouth dropped open. After seeing Jake in his state of undress, and arousal, she'd forgotten all about what she was wearing. Or rather, what she wasn't. She had on exactly what she'd worn to bed—a tiny pair of French-cut bikini panties and her thin camisole. There was far more of her showing than was covered.

Far, far more.

And every inch of her body was tingling.

Chapter Five

"Misfired shots," Jake repeated under his breath. He gulped down some coffee, hoping it would ease the pounding in his head. "From a robbery attempt nearby."

Jake hung up the phone, the police officer's words still ringing in his ears. A wrong place at the wrong time kind of theory. He didn't tell the detective that he didn't buy that. Too many things just didn't make sense about the shooting, and it wasn't a case of misfired shots.

"There you are." Willa hurried into the kitchen, where he stood, his gaze still aimed at the phone he'd just hung up. "We heard on the news that someone fired shots at you. Why the devil didn't you call us?"

"Are you all right, Jake?" Douglas asked, coming in right behind her.

Jake had anticipated their visit, just not quite this soon. "The gunman wasn't shooting at me," he clarified. "I think he was shooting at Jessie."

"Jessie?" Douglas and Willa repeated in unison.

This explanation would have to come eventually. He'd counted on it happening later, after a half-dozen cups of coffee, but there was no reason to put it off.

Any minute, Jessie would probably walk through that door. Hopefully, she'd be wearing more than she had been on the previous night. If not, his tongue would land on the floor and he wouldn't be capable of explaining anything.

One thing was for sure, Jessie Barrett didn't look like a pregnant woman. That was the fourth thing Jake had noticed about her after she'd stepped onto the balcony the night before. The first three things that had caught his attention were her breasts and trim little butt. He would have had to be blind not to notice those things.

And not respond to them.

She had worn a thin little white top that he supposed substituted for a bra. He'd seen the outline of her breasts and her tightly budded nipples. Her breasts had jiggled a little when she walked and swayed against the tight fabric.

A specific part of him had appreciated the groin-tightening view. Greatly appreciated it. It was his brain that was still giving him some trouble.

She was off-limits. There were just too many things he didn't know about her. And too many that he did. Like, she was pregnant, for instance.

His body had a strange reaction to that reminder. Jake had suddenly wanted nothing more than to lay her on that floor and sink into her. He wanted to hear Jessie whisper his name. He wanted her scent on him. And his on her. He wanted to feel her shatter around him while he was deep inside her.

All in all, he was disgusted with himself. It was just as well that she'd hightailed it off the balcony. He shouldn't have those kinds of thoughts about her. Once they figured out who was behind all of this, then…well, he didn't even know what would happen. But he sure couldn't fantasize about having sex with her on his balcony. He couldn't fantasize about having sex with her anywhere.

"Jessie's someone I met," Jake explained, giving them the short, sanitized version, which included only a small amount of information. "She's having a few problems, so she'll stay here for a while."

They looked at him as if he'd sprouted feathers. With good reason. He hadn't brought a woman home since Anne.

"Have we met this Jessie?" Willa asked. Her blue eyes, a genetic match of his own, were wide with concern.

Jake drank more coffee and shook his head. Thank God, he could already feel the caffeine working. "No."

Douglas shook his head, too, and accepted the cup of coffee that Ellen handed him. After serving Willa some tea, the housekeeper excused herself and left the room.

"This doesn't sound good, Jake," Douglas said pensively. "How long have you known this woman?"

"Not long."

Douglas swore under his breath. "And you brought her home with you?"

"Like I said, she's having some problems—"

"Problems you don't need. We're three-and-a-half months from election day, for Christ's sake. You don't need this kind of distraction from some woman."

For some reason, that remark riled Jake. "Funny,

a few days ago you encouraged me to bed Rawley Emmett's wife.''

Douglas caught Jake's arm. ''So that's what this is about—sex?''

''Hell, no.'' He would have denied it more adamantly if at that exact moment Jessie hadn't walked into the room.

She paused at the doorway, eyeing Douglas and Willa much as she'd eyed the guard dogs the night before. ''I'm sorry. I've interrupted a family meeting.''

''Jessie?'' Willa questioned. And there was more than just enquiry in her voice. Jake detected some jealousy, as well. It was a knee-jerk reaction on his sister's part. She'd learned the hard way to be jealous of any attractive woman within a hundred yards of her husband.

But there was nothing lascivious in Douglas's gaze. He just stared at Jessie, using an abrasive scowl that Jake had seen him toss at anybody he thought might get in his way or the way of the election. Douglas was a tenacious campaign manager, but he could be brutal with contingencies. Jessie was the ultimate contingency.

Or she easily could be.

Jake glanced at Jessie. She looked ready to faint. Obviously, she hadn't intended to face anyone but Ellen and him this morning. Maybe she wouldn't blurt out anything about the kidnapping and insemination before he could stop her. Knowing he needed to do something, anything, he crossed the room to her.

''I'm sorry,'' she murmured. ''I didn't know they would—''

Jake lowered his head and put his mouth on hers. It was quick, a borderline peck, and he pulled back fully expecting that Jessie might slap him into the next county. She didn't. A soft breath rumbled in her throat.

"Why did you do that?" she whispered, her voice a strangled protest.

"Because we'll have to pretend we're lovers or else answer a ton of questions I don't want to answer. Understand?"

She paused. Blinked. "Yes."

Finally, Jake heard some grit in her voice. She wasn't as pale this morning, either, but there were still faint circles under her eyes. No makeup. Just a scrubbed-clean face that made Jessie look wholesome. Well, except for that hair. It seemed to jut out in every direction.

Her clothes were different. She had on jeans, slim and snug, and a white shirt she had knotted at the waist. Ellen had probably come up with the outfit. He wouldn't exactly thank his housekeeper for it. Underneath the white shirt, he could tell Jessie had on a little top similar to the one he'd gotten a good look at the night before. It was somehow sexier than all the flimsy undergarments he'd ever seen.

Jessie leaned closer and kept her voice at a harsh whisper. "Just don't kiss me again."

"Even if it's all for show?"

That seemed to annoy her. Or something. Jake couldn't figure out why she wrinkled her nose and frowned. "My hormones are all out of whack, I guess."

"Beg your pardon?"

Her gaze darted uncomfortably around the room

before it returned to his. She cleared her throat, and for the first time since he'd met her, Jake saw some vulnerability in her pale gray eyes. Strange, he hadn't seen that when the gunman was firing at them.

"Uh, my hormones haven't figured out it's all for show, okay?" Her voice actually cracked. "So just leave the kissing out of this."

Speechless, Jake stared at her for a moment. She had actually responded to that little kiss? And she'd admitted it? To him, no less. Well, he wouldn't dwell on the fact that the kiss had sent certain parts of his body into overdrive, either. No. This attraction that simmered between them would just have to quit.

He circled his arm around her, felt her body tense and brought her into the kitchen for introductions. "Jessie, this is my sister, Willa, and her husband, Douglas Harland. Douglas is also my campaign manager."

No one commented for several snail-crawling moments, but some uncomfortable glances passed between Willa and Douglas.

Jessie finally stepped closer. "It's nice to meet you. I'll just make myself a cup of tea or something and then get out of your way."

"No need to leave," Douglas said icily. "Jake was just telling us all about you before you came in."

"Well…" And probably because she didn't know what else to do, Jessie shrugged. "That's nice."

"Nice, my foot." Willa gave her husband a scolding glance. "Jake hasn't told us anything other than that the two of you recently met. That hardly qualifies as 'all about you.' I thought maybe you could fill us in where he left off."

But Jake didn't get a chance to run interference for Jessie. Outside, he heard the dogs barking, and he quickly crossed the room to the window. Barreling up the road was an oversize black luxury car, and the Dobermans were in hot pursuit.

Jessie joined him at the window. "Someone you know?" she asked in a frantic whisper.

"No." He didn't take the time to soothe the terrified expression that took control of her. He made eye contact with his sister. "We have a problem. Take Jessie and Ellen to my office, and lock the door. Then call the security company and ask them why they didn't respond to a breach at the gate."

The three had already started to move, when the phone rang. Without taking his eyes off the approaching car, Jake snatched it up. "McClendon."

"Call off your dogs," the man snarled. "This is Abel Markham and we need to talk."

Markham. He was absolutely the last person Jake expected to see this morning. "How'd you get through the gate?"

"It was wide open." The car came to a screeching stop in front of the house. "Now call off those dogs." And with that order, he hung up.

"It's Markham," Jake relayed. "He wants to talk."

"I must have forgotten to close the gate when I drove through," Willa volunteered. "Sorry."

The lapse in security didn't please Jake, but he'd deal with that later. Right now he had a more urgent problem on his hands. Curiosity alone was enough to prompt him to see Markham. But this was about more that just plain curiosity. Maybe this was the first step in getting some answers about who'd fired those shots.

Jake turned to Jessie. It didn't take a mind reader to know she didn't want to be left alone with Willa and Douglas. The alternative was going with him. If Markham was behind the plot, then Jake didn't think it was a good idea for them to be in the same room. Especially if Jessie didn't have anything to do with the scheme. And if she did have something to do with it, well, it was pretty obvious that her conspirator now wanted her dead. So it was best if she stayed put.

"I won't be long," he said.

"But what if—"

He shook his head, cutting her off. "Markham's not going to do anything stupid with this many witnesses around." But he wasn't nearly as confident as he hoped he sounded. The truth was, he didn't know what was about to happen. But one thing was for sure: he planned to be armed.

"I'm coming with you," Douglas insisted.

Jake didn't waste time trying to talk him out of it. He stopped by the hall closet, took a gun from the top shelf and slipped it into the back waist of his jeans. "Just a precaution," he told Douglas when he noted the renewed look of concern in his eyes.

The moment Jake stepped outside, he signaled the dogs. As they'd been trained to do, they immediately stopped barking and eased away from the car. However, they didn't leave. They came onto the porch and stood like vigilant sentries next to Douglas and him.

Markham stepped out from the car. He was alone and obviously furious. He stomped up the steps, his meaty hands clenched in fists at his side, his polished shoes smacking against the limestone. His face was flushed, making the tiny broken veins on his nose even more noticeable.

"What the hell are you trying to do to me?" Markham bellowed.

"Beat you in an election?" Jake could tell that wasn't the answer his political opponent wanted to hear. "Why are you here?"

The man stopped a few inches away. He was so close, Jake could smell his breath. Coffee laced with whiskey. "You know why. You set the cops on me. They called last night to talk to me about some shots that you say were fired at you."

Evidently, Markham hadn't heard the cop's latest theory about the botched robbery. Jake wouldn't mention it to his guest. He would let Markham stew a little longer.

"The police think you had something to do with that?" Douglas asked.

"No! Hell, no! They're just acting on Mc-Clendon's word. Or maybe yours. Well, I'm here to tell you both to call them off. I won't have my good name dragged through the mud by some little piss-ants like you."

"Your name's already been dragged through the mud," Jake calmly reminded him. "Between the big payoffs from the special-interest groups and your questionable campaign funds, you've got mud all over your name. That's why I'm running against you. And that's the reason I'll win. The days of good-old-boy politics are over."

"They're not over and neither is this." He jammed his finger against Jake's chest. "If you mention my name in the same breath as you do this shooting, then I'll sue you for every penny you've got.''

Jake knocked Markham's hand away, but it was Douglas who answered. ''Maybe we should sue you when you bring up that woman that they found dead on Jake's property last year. Every chance you get, you remind the media about Christy Mendoza's death, and you know Jake didn't have a thing to do with that. It was an accident.''

Markham smiled. ''I don't know that. How do I know my worthy opponent isn't into hurting women? Everybody knows he practically killed his wife when he talked her into having that baby. Of course, his daddy's will made it hard for him to pass up all that money. A man who'd want a kid just to collect a trust fund—''

''Careful.'' Jake's voice dropped. ''You don't want to go there, Markham. Ever. This visit is over. If you're still here in thirty seconds, the dogs will consider you an intruder and attack.'' He turned and started back inside. He didn't get far.

Jessie was in the foyer, and from the wary look on her face, Jake realized she'd heard at least part of the conversation. Definitely the last part. And that was something he hadn't wanted her to hear.

''Is everything all right?'' she asked, her voice brittle.

''Fine. Markham was just leaving.''

Jake followed Jessie's suddenly fixed gaze to the man on the porch. A malicious smile shoved up the corner of Markham's thin mouth when he gave Jessie a long, lingering look. And with that smile still in place, Abel Markham strolled back to his car.

Chapter Six

Jessie stood in the living room and watched as Jake said goodbye to Willa and Douglas. He'd been borderline rude in insisting they leave. Still, she didn't blame him. The morning hadn't gotten off to a good start with their visit and then Markham's arrival. Combined with the awful night they'd had, Jake had probably reached his limit.

She certainly had.

The pretend kiss hadn't helped. It had done funny things to her body. Jessie tried to blame those *funny things* on the pregnancy, but it wasn't her condition causing it. This was some kind of spooky attraction to a man she shouldn't be attracted to in any way, shape or form. There was just one problem. She didn't know how to make it stop.

''Are you all right?'' Jake asked, walking toward her.

Only then did Jessie realize she'd been staring at him. And there was certainly a lot of him to stare at. He was every bit the cowboy. Jeans, worn white in places she wished weren't so obvious, particularly around the zipper area. Boots, scuffed on the toes. A blue cotton shirt that showed nearly every muscle the man had.

"I just have a headache," she answered while she quickly tried to regroup. He already believed she was a possible criminal. Best not to let him think she was stupid, as well. "So Markham's the man that you believe is behind this?"

"It's a strong possibility." He caught her hand and led her to a comfortable, overstuffed chair. "Did you recognize his voice?"

"No. He wasn't one of the men at the warehouse." She felt a dizzy spell coming on. Or some kind of spell. Unfortunately, whenever she was near Jake, her body seemed to malfunction. It didn't help when he put his hand on the back of her neck. "What are you doing?"

"Trying to help you get rid of that headache." He began to massage her stiff neck muscles. Jessie sighed before she could stop herself.

"About Markham," Jake continued. "No weird feelings about him being connected to what happened?"

"No. Not really." But there was no way Jessie could pass up the opportunity Markham had given her to ask about Christy's death. "I heard him mention the woman who died here at the ranch. Since she worked at the cantina, maybe he's trying to connect you with her death. And mine. The authorities would probably dig hard if two of Ray's employees ended up dead and both were somehow connected to you."

"But then we're back to why would Markham go through the trouble of having you inseminated?"

"I don't know. Maybe some psychological ploy

to get to you. And maybe your vials really were destroyed at Cryogen. Perhaps Markham had the kidnappers mention your name so I'd go to the cops with it.''

Of course, that didn't explain why Markham would want her dead.

''Speaking of the cops, they called this morning,'' he calmly stated. ''They think those shots fired at us yesterday were all a mistake. A robbery took place nearby.''

Jessie let that sink in. It didn't sink in well. ''So they're not really going to investigate it?''

His fingers stilled. ''They didn't say that specifically, but I got the impression such an investigation wouldn't be a top priority.''

''And my kidnapping?''

''They stopped by the warehouse where you told them you were held. Nothing. It was empty and apparently hasn't been used in years. The cops said they would continue to look into it.'' He started the massage again. A little lower, though. He worked his fingers inside the collar of her shirt.

Jessie shook her head in frustration. ''But you don't really think they will, because I'm just a cocktail waitress with a far-fetched story?''

''They didn't say that.''

''No, but that's what they're thinking.'' It made her want to phone the police and tell them everything. Of course, it probably wouldn't do any good. She truly didn't know anything that would lead them to the person behind this plan to kill her.

''My security people came up with some information on Dr. Radelman,'' he continued. ''He just started a six-month project in South America. He can't even be reached by phone.''

She blew out a long breath. ''Well, that's convenient. I guess his boss figures I'll be dead before then.''

''But apparently Dr. Radelman still has a house here in San Antonio. He's not married. No family nearby. It's also for sale. So that means the house will be empty.''

That got her attention. ''And?''

''I thought I might like to have a look around it. Tonight.''

Jessie angled her head and looked back at him. This wasn't some empty gesture on his part. A guy like Jake didn't go prowling around a stranger's house unless he had reason to think he'd find something. ''Are you starting to believe what I told you?''

''Maybe. Some parts of it, anyway.''

But he still didn't trust her. Jessie heard that loud and clear. It was just as well. She didn't trust him, either.

It did drive home a point, though—she desperately needed someone on her side. She needed a friend, and there was only one person who fit that bill. Just as soon as she could get a few minutes to herself, she would call Byron.

Jake walked around the front of her chair and dropped down onto the leather ottoman only a few inches from her knees. The new position put them nearly face-to-face. And eye-to-eye. Since Jessie didn't care for that, she decided to get his baby blues to focus on something else.

''Say, while you're down there, I have a cramp in

the arch of my right foot. Why don't you put those magic fingers to good use?''

He didn't hesitate. Jake pulled her foot into his lap, put her strappy sandal aside and got to work. Jessie leaned her head back on the chair and smiled before she could stop herself. ''I think you missed your calling, McClendon. You should have been a masseur.''

''I'll keep that in mind if the political career doesn't work out.'' His fingers continued to circle her arch. ''By the way, have you given any thought to the baby?''

She tensed up again. Great. Why had he brought up the baby now? ''It's hard not to think about it.''

He made a sound of agreement. Paused. And then repeated the sound. ''Will you actually carry it to term?''

''Of course.''

Jessie hadn't even considered an alternative. And wouldn't. It was odd. Aside from Christy and Byron, there was no one she'd felt truly connected to. But there was a connection with this child. And it was already so incredibly strong, so permanent, so real that it seemed as if this tiny, precious life had always been there. There were no limits to that kind of love. And no limits to what she would do to protect her baby.

''But what about the circumstances of the conception?'' he asked.

That wasn't idle curiosity in his voice. Nor was it the question of a man trying to work out the details of the sinister plan that had thrown them together. There was genuine concern in his eyes.

"Call it my personal convictions—whatever. I'll have this child."

"And afterward? After it's born?"

Jessie took a deep breath. "I haven't thought beyond that. I never planned to have kids. Heck, I never even wanted to get married."

"Why not?"

She started to say nothing about her childhood. That's what she had always done when people asked, but it didn't work this time. Jessie wanted him to hear the ugly truth—maybe that would put some emotional distance back between them. This odd sort of closeness wasn't something she wanted to feel.

"My father was a worthless excuse for a human being who used to beat my mother just to prove to her how much he loved her. I decided when I was a kid that I didn't want any man to have that kind of control over me. Besides, I can have this child on my own. I have a little money put aside and I'll do what's necessary."

"Just like that?" His eyes skimmed over her. "You've made up your mind about this baby so soon? You only found out for sure that you were pregnant yesterday."

That seemed a lifetime ago. She'd aged a dozen years overnight.

"My decision has nothing to do with how much time has passed." Her breath caught, when he rubbed a sensitive spot on her foot. "It's a decision of the heart. Not very rational, I know. Still, it's the only decision I can live with."

When the massage abruptly stopped, Jessie lifted her head. He was staring at her. "Have you felt the baby move?"

"I think it's too soon for that. The only thing I feel is a sort of pressure in my lower abdomen." She slid her hand over the spot. "It doesn't hurt or anything. I'm just aware of it."

"Here—?" He reached out and placed his hand over hers. It was probably a mistake, but she looked at him again. Their gazes met. Held. That unwavering, almost pleading look in his eyes caused her breath to stall in her throat. Slowly, she pulled back her hand, leaving only his warm palm on her stomach. He kept it there a second, then two, before he eased it away.

"Water," Jessie finally managed to say. "I'd like a glass of water." She had already started to get to her feet, but Jake simply put his hand on her shoulder.

"I'll get it." He rose and went to the bar. Silently, he stood there for a moment, his back to her, before he opened a bottle of water and poured it into a glass.

Something had just happened. Jessie was sure of it. But what? And did she want to know? No, she finally decided. After looking at Jake's still uneasy expression, she knew she definitely wanted him to keep his thoughts to himself.

IT WAS HIS CHILD.

Jake knew it. He just didn't know *how* he knew it.

God. A baby. *His* baby. He handed Jessie her water and quickly walked back to the window. He couldn't face her yet. He had to steady his heart first.

He'd accused her of lying, of trying to con him. Maybe she was, but if so the con didn't extend to the child she carried. No, that part of her story was real.

The baby was real.

He braced his hands on the bar and took a deep breath. He had to get out of there, away from her. He needed some time to think. "I have to go out for a while. Errands. I'll probably be gone most of the afternoon. Tomorrow, I'd like to have a doctor examine you." He waited for Jessie to object. She didn't. She didn't say anything. "You can trust this man. I've known him for years."

"Good." Her voice was soft and small.

Did she sense something was wrong? He hoped not.

"The doctor will want a medical history," Jake continued. His grip tightened on the bar. "You should probably tell him you were inseminated and how they did the procedure." He glanced at her over his shoulder. "Did they do all of this in that warehouse?"

"Yes." She cleared her throat and repeated the response to give it some sound. "But they'd fixed up a section to look more like a cell. Padded walls. Locks. They kept a guard posted outside the door at all times."

That wasn't the easiest description for him to hear. "Did you ever try to escape?"

"Of course. Several times. Once I even braided my hair and tried to use it to put the guard in a choke hold. It didn't work. He just backhanded me and then cut off my hair."

Jake cursed under his breath. Such violent beginnings for the conception of his child. If she was telling the truth, then it was almost as if she'd been raped.

"Anyway, I did escape the day I heard them say they were going to, um, kill me," Jessie continued. She stumbled over her words. "They gave me a shot, and I pretended it hit me fast. I was woozy, but I guess they thought I was completely out of it. For whatever reason, they didn't lock the door, so I got out of there as fast as I could. I hid in a Dumpster for a while. That's when I saw the newspaper that said you'd be at the Riverwalk Hotel."

And she had gone there and broken into his suite. As difficult as this was for him to hear, Jake knew he needed to know. "When did you first realize they planned to inseminate you?"

"I kept hearing them mention 'cryovials' and 'nitro-preservation solution,' but I didn't understand what they meant. I knew they were examining me for something. They'd send in one of the men to hold me down while they took blood. They gave me a gynecological exam. A couple of days after that, they brought in that vial, and I figured out what it was."

His theory about Markham actually started to make sense. Too bad he didn't know for sure what part Jessie played in it.

"So let me get this straight," she said, drawing his attention back to her. "You want me to tell the doctor everything but the name on the vial they used to inseminate me?"

That was it in a nutshell. It seemed stupid to keep something like that from Dr. Lisette, but Jake wasn't ready to announce to the world that Jessie was carrying his child.

He nodded and left.

Chapter Seven

There was a long silence on the line after Jessie told Byron about the shots that someone had fired at her. She let him rant for a while about how she could have been killed and about how irresponsible Jake McClendon was to have let her go out like that in the first place. It didn't do any good to remind him that Jake had risked his life to save her and that it was Jake who had ultimately gotten them to safety.

After a litany of Byron's colorful insults, she hit him with even more shocking news—she told him about the kidnapping and the insemination. And then the pregnancy.

"Hell," Byron finally mumbled.

Well, that wasn't the way she felt about the pregnancy, but it did aptly describe her situation. There was a killer out there somewhere, and he wanted her and her baby dead. Somehow, some way, she'd get to the bottom of all of this.

Jessie glanced at the clock, something she'd done several times during her conversation with Byron. She had already been on the line twenty minutes and didn't dare risk much more. After all, she was making the call from Jake's house. He wasn't there, of course, he was out doing some errands. Still, she didn't want his housekeeper to hear any part of this conversation.

"What about the money?" Jessie asked.

As if he were pulling himself out of deep thought, it took Byron a moment to answer. "I should have it day after tomorrow. I'll bring it to you."

"Definitely not a good idea." For about a million reasons. Half of those reasons had to do with her host. "I'll do a pickup the way we planned it."

"Does McClendon know?" Byron demanded.

"About the pregnancy, yes."

"No." He made a frustrated groan. "Does he know you're a cop?"

"A former cop," she automatically corrected.

Byron didn't even pause. "A cop on an extended leave of absence. You can return to the department anytime you want."

That wasn't exactly true. Technically, she was a renegade, an officer who had conducted an investigation into her friend's death, which she'd been ordered not to do. Returning would mean disciplinary action. Besides, she couldn't return pregnant.

"Jake doesn't know I'm a cop," she finally answered. "And I want to keep it that way for a while." For how long, Jessie didn't know. It just didn't seem like the right time to tell him she'd been conducting an unauthorized investigation that involved him. She already had enough to deal with.

Byron cursed. "So he doesn't know you're looking into Christy's death?"

"No." Christy had died on Jake's property, so at least Jessie was near the scene of the crime. Months earlier, she'd been convinced that her friend had been murdered. In fact, she had sworn at Christy's funeral that she would make someone pay. That someone, she'd thought, was Jake.

Jessie easily recalled the last conversation she'd ever had with Christy. She'd gone over it so many times, trying to hang on to every precious word, all the while trying to sift through it for clues. *A tough job, but hey, someone has to do it,* Christy had said, after explaining that she would be at the McClendon ranch later that night. And Christy had laughed in that carefree way of hers and called Jake a cowboy sizzler. Jessie rarely agreed with Christy about her choice in men, but in this one case, her friend had been right.

She smiled at the memory, but at the same time it made her eyes misty. Many times Jessie had wished she had that moment back so she could try to convince Christy to return to Austin. To return home to the apartment they'd shared for years prior to Christy taking the job in San Antonio. If Jessie had convinced her to return, her friend would still be alive.

"Jessie, are you still there?" she heard Byron ask. At the sound of his voice, the image of Christy began to vanish. That smiling heart-shaped face framed with a thick mane of chestnut hair. Jessie tried to hang on to it a moment longer, but she couldn't. The image faded, leaving only the ache in Jessie's heart.

"I'm here," she replied. "I was just thinking about Christy."

"Yeah." And the pause let her know he was thinking of their mutual friend, as well. "I miss her a lot."

"I know you do." The pain she heard in Byron's voice made Jessie ache even more. After all, Byron had been in love with Christy. Not that Christy had returned those feelings, but thankfully she'd always been sensitive to the way he felt. Deep inside, Jessie had always prayed that Christy would come to her senses and return Byron's love. And it might have happened eventually, if Christy hadn't died.

"Did you hear me, Jess?" Byron asked.

"No. What did you say?"

"I said you could be in the house right now with the man who wants to kill you."

Jessie didn't believe that any longer. After all, if Jake had truly wanted her dead, he'd already had ample opportunity. He could have shot her after she passed out in his hotel suite. The cops would have dismissed it as a man protecting himself against an intruder. Or he could have killed her once he'd broken into her motel room. Again, he could have found a way to cover his tracks. But instead, it seemed as if he wanted to get to the truth as much as she did.

"By the way, Jake ran a fingerprint check on me," Jessie said so she wouldn't have to address Byron's other comment. "He got my real name, but the cover held. That rap sheet was a nice touch. You didn't tell me you were going to add that."

"Rap sheets are easier to create than most other records. You said to give you a past, and I did."

Yes, he had. Now Jake thought she was a first-class loser. That bothered her. Still, it was better than the alternative.

"Please tell me you have a plan to find out what's going on," Byron said.

Well, it wasn't much of a plan, but it was all she had. "Jake and I are going to check out Dr. Radelman's house tonight."

"Oh, Jess. That's not a good idea, not after someone fired those shots at you. You've got to rethink that. Anything could happen if you go there."

The slight sound alerted her. A *click,* as if someone had picked up on another line. Jessie's heart stopped. She listened for another click to indicate the person had hung up. It didn't happen. In fact, she heard breathing. Someone was trying to listen in on her conversation. Jake, maybe? But he'd said he would be out most of the afternoon. It was barely one o'clock.

"I have to go," she said abruptly to Byron.

"No. Please, rethink this—"

"I'll call you when I can."

She slammed down the phone and raced out of the room. Not that she knew where to look. The size of the house would probably make it impossible to find the person who'd been on the other line.

Jessie felt the rapid pounding of her heart as she darted down the hallway. One by one she threw open doors, glanced inside the rooms and moved on to the next. With each step, she fought to control the torrent that shot through her. Had Byron been right? Was she in the house with a killer? Of course, even if Jake had tried to eavesdrop, it didn't mean he wanted her dead. There was something about the listener, something about that *click* that had caused an icy shiver to go down her spine.

From the doorway of the library, she detected some movement in the far corner and, again, reached for a gun that wasn't there. Jessie bit back a groan of frustration and braced herself to fight.

Or to flee.

Another image slashed through her mind, an image

as clear and as provoking as Christy's had been earlier. Her baby. The tiny baby that she carried inside
her. Even if she won a fight, the baby might be hurt.
Just the thought of that nearly brought her to her
knees. All her police training meant nothing because
it couldn't assure the safety of her child.

Jessie felt a cold film of perspiration on her skin.
Felt the muscles in her body tremble from the tight
strain. With her breath held, she took another look
inside the room. And saw the man in the darkened
corner.

Not Jake. *Douglas.*

He didn't say a word, but even in the nearly dark
room she instinctively knew he had his gaze pinned
to her. There was a phone on the table next to him.
Had he been the one to eavesdrop?

"Jessie," he greeted her. Strange, she'd never gotten a chill before when someone said her name, but
she did now. The man obviously detested her. With
reason. He likely saw her as a potential problem for
Jake's campaign. At least, she hoped that was all
there was to it.

Douglas switched on the light and lifted his nearly
empty glass. "Care for a drink?"

She shook her head. Her every instinct screamed
for her to step back, but she held her ground. "Were
you just on the phone?" she asked.

He looked at it as if just noticing it was there.
"Nope. Not me. Come in. I was hoping we'd have
a chance to talk."

Jessie didn't intend to get any closer to him than
she already was, and she didn't believe him. She
would bet money on the fact he'd been the one on
the line. What she couldn't figure out was why he'd

lied. Douglas didn't appear to be the sort who worried about covering his tracks.

"Talk about what?" she asked, trying to force herself to breathe normally. It didn't work.

The fact that her voice cracked seemed to amuse him. He smiled and pointed to a framed photograph that was next to the phone. "See this? That was Anne, Jake's wife."

It was a casual shot of a sleek blonde standing next to Willa. Jake's sister had a hunting rifle propped on her shoulder and Anne held up a plate-shaped trophy. Both women were smiling. One glimpse and she could see that Anne was everything Jessie knew she wasn't. Beautiful, busty and dripping with class. It was easy to see why Jake had married her.

"Anne died four years ago," Douglas continued, his hand tightening on the crystal whiskey glass. "Care to guess how many women Jake's brought here since then?"

No, Jessie didn't want to guess. She could tell from Douglas's suddenly ruffled expression what the answer was.

"None," Douglas provided. "Well, except for you. And that's what I'm trying to figure out. Why you?"

She moved her shoulder, an indifferent shrug, but inside she had no feelings of indifference. She wanted to get away from this man as quickly as possible. He was dangerous, and she could feel that in every fiber of her body. Jessie turned to leave, but what Douglas said next stopped her in her tracks.

"The gossips had a field day with Jake after Anne died," he continued, his voice low as if telling a secret. "Large sums of money always get tongues wagging. Some people thought Jake wanted a child simply so he could inherit the millions that his parents left in a trust fund for their grandchildren.''

This was the first Jessie had heard about a trust fund, but she remembered Markham mentioning something about money in a will. She slowly turned back to face Douglas. "Are there any grandchildren?"

"No. Willa and I tried for years, but once she was past forty, we thought it was time to give up."

Jessie gripped on the door frame, hoping it would steady her trembling hands. "But Jake, uh, could always have children."

"I doubt it. I don't think he'd want to risk it again after what happened to Anne. That always seems to be the way, doesn't it? The people who want them can't have them. Other people can turn one out every nine months."

And sometimes people, like her, didn't have any say in the matter. "So what will happen to this trust fund?"

"In about three weeks, on Jake's thirty-fifth birthday, it'll be divided between Willa and him. Not that Jake needs the money, but Willa and I would like to start our own business." The clever smile returned. "Does Jake's bank account interest you, Jessie?"

She felt as if he'd struck her. Douglas had obviously misinterpreted the reasons for her questions. Her concern had been for Jake, for a possible motive in all of this, not his money.

Jessie jerked her hands from the door frame and folded her arms over her chest. "No. Why would it?"

He took a step toward her. One calculated, slow,

soundless step. His smile slipped away as quickly as it had come. Douglas pulled his mouth into a flat line. His nostrils flared. He reminded Jessie of a wild animal whose territory had just been violated. And she was obviously the violator.

"Consider this a warning, Jessie. The only one you'll get." His words were like cold steel slamming against glass. "Find a way to distance yourself from Jake and do it soon."

The challenge both frightened and infuriated her. She certainly hadn't asked to be part of Jake's life. Just the opposite. Besides, she didn't think Jake would appreciate anyone, including Douglas, speaking for him.

Protectively, she slid her hand over her stomach. "And if I don't distance myself?"

He tossed back the rest of his whiskey. "It's my job to eliminate obstacles to the campaign."

That's obviously what Douglas thought she was. Something to be eliminated. And if he felt that way, perhaps Willa did, too.

The sheer callousness in his warning robbed Jessie of her breath. She took the step back that she'd fought taking from the moment she had first seen Douglas in the room.

"I'll keep that in mind," she said as she turned and left.

While she was at it, she would keep something else in mind. She wasn't safe just because she was on the ranch. After all, Markham had gotten through. And now Douglas had issued that not-so-veiled threat. It was a brutal reminder that she needed to find some answers fast. Maybe then, she could finally get her baby and herself to safety.

Jake saw Jessie when she started down the hall away from where Willa and he had come to a standstill. She obviously didn't see them, and she was also obviously in a hurry. It made him thankful he'd returned early from his "errands." Maybe he could find out what was going on.

A moment later, Douglas stepped into the doorway. He didn't look in their direction, either. He kept his attention focused right on Jessie, watching her, until she disappeared into her room. Jake saw an insidious smile lift the corner of Douglas's mouth. Willa no doubt saw it, as well. Jake heard her whisper-soft gasp.

He caught his sister's hand, well aware of what was going through her mind. Heck, he didn't blame her. She'd recounted to him at least a half-dozen of Douglas's extra-marital affairs. And even with such behavior, which Jake found reprehensible, Willa would be the first to declare her love for her husband. Jake admired his brother-in-law's business sense, but he'd always secretly hoped that Willa would see the light and order her husband out of her life.

"If Jessie has…" But Willa didn't finish.

"She wouldn't do that," Jake quickly assured her in a voice soft enough that Douglas wouldn't hear. He wanted to watch his brother-in-law a moment longer.

"And how do you know that, huh? Douglas had her checked out, and he told me she worked at that seedy club in San Antonio."

The shock hit Jake with full force. It felt as if his stomach had turned to stone. "Douglas did that?" He barely kept his voice even. Hard to do with the burst of anger he suddenly felt. How dare Douglas go behind his back to investigate Jessie.

"That other woman, Christy Mendoza, worked there, too," Willa added.

At the sound of Willa's raised voice, Douglas's gaze whipped in their direction. The smile evaporated, and catlike he walked toward them.

Willa jerked her hand from Jake's grip and made an angry shivering sound while she stormed toward Douglas. "Please tell me you're not trying to start something with that woman."

Douglas seemed only mildly concerned with Willa's fury. "It never crossed my mind," he said almost sarcastically.

"That's bull. You were just looking at Jessie the way you looked at that other woman who worked at the same club."

Jake had already opened his mouth to excuse himself from this argument and to insist that Douglas meet with him in private to discuss his background check on Jessie. That, however, stopped him cold.

"What do you mean, Willa?" Jake kept his eyes on Douglas, though, when he asked his sister that question.

"I mean, he followed that woman around half the night." She added some profanity under her breath. "God, he practically drooled on himself."

Still no reaction from Douglas. He stayed eerily calm. And that bothered Jake more than any outburst or angry denial would have done.

"Willa, you're imagining things again," Douglas explained almost dispassionately. "Jake knows about my past indiscretions, but that's all behind me. In fact, he made me swear to it before he accepted my offer to be his campaign manager. Isn't that right, Jake?''

It was true, but Jake had no idea if Douglas had kept his word. And since the patina of politeness had disappeared, Jake decided not to pull any punches. ''I don't want you investigating Jessie—got that?''

Now Douglas had a reaction. Annoyance danced through his raisin-colored eyes. ''But she—''

''You had no right,'' Jake interrupted. He turned to leave, saying the rest of what he had to say over his shoulder. ''And it won't happen again.''

Chapter Eight

Jessie finally won the argument with Jake.

No easy feat.

She'd insisted that she accompany him to Dr. Radelman's house. Jake hadn't wanted her to go—because of her safety, he'd said. Jessie dug in her heels and reminded him that she might recognize something they could use against Radelman. Finally, she wore him down, and he agreed to let her go.

Now as they parked up the street from the house, she conceded that Jake had a point about safety. Specifically, the baby's safety. She couldn't keep doing things that could put her life, and therefore the child's, in danger.

Of course, doing nothing might prove just as dangerous.

"How exactly will we get in?" she asked, eyeing the houses that lined both sides of the suburban street. It was a Neighborhood Watch kind of area, and she didn't relish the idea of breaking in.

He dangled a key in front of her. "This way."

"Where did you get that?"

"Douglas. He knows the owner of the real estate agency that Radelman's using to sell his house."

"Convenient."

He lifted a shoulder. "I didn't tell Douglas why I needed it. I figured it was best to leave him out of this."

Jessie quietly agreed. As far as she was concerned, she wanted Douglas to have nothing to do with anything going on in her life. Their little chat still had her shaken.

Jake pointed his finger at her. "All right, here's the deal, and if you don't agree, I'll take you right back to the ranch. If anything—and I mean *anything*—goes wrong, you'll get out of there without arguing. First sign of trouble, I want you gone." He waited until she nodded in agreement. "Then, let's get this over with."

It certainly didn't look like the residence of a felon. There was a cobblestone walkway, tan shutters, ornate grillwork on the porch and flowers. Even in the pale streetlight, Jessie could see the tiny blue buds that dotted the thick rosemary bushes in front of the house.

Jake unlocked the door, and they slipped inside. He clicked on a tiny flashlight that he took from the pocket of his windbreaker. "Stay right with me," he whispered, handing her a pair of thin rubber gloves, also from his pocket. He put on a pair himself. "And if we find anything, we'll call the cops. The idea isn't to tamper with evidence here."

She rolled her eyes. Jessie didn't have that in mind, either. What she wanted, though, was to find solid proof and stop the person who had kidnapped her.

Their search was slow and tedious because of the near darkness, and because Jessie had no idea what they were looking for. Still, they checked the obvious places, all the drawers and closets. Then they checked the not-so-obvious ones, including the toilet tanks.

The place was clean. Too clean. Radelman's furniture was still there, but there weren't any personal items lying around. No photos. No mementos of any kind. Even the drawer to his nightstand was empty, and there wasn't so much as a trace of lint in the pockets of the clothes that hung in his closet. Someone had obviously sanitized everything.

Jessie was ready to give up, when she glanced again at the notepad on the desk. The top sheet was blank, but she thumbed through it. On the second-last page, she found some writing.

"Seems to be a list," Jake observed from over her shoulder. He held the flashlight so they could read it. "Transport kit for aliquots. Storage tank."

"Aliquots," Jessie repeated. "Samples. Specifically, equal samples of something. Perhaps yours." She glanced up at him when he didn't say anything. He was staring at her. "What?"

"Since when does a cocktail waitress need to know about aliquots?"

Jessie flinched. What a stupid thing for her to say. But she didn't panic. She quickly covered her tracks. "A cocktail waitress doesn't need to know it, but I do own a dictionary. And I use it on occasion."

"Then, do you have any idea what that is—?" Jake pointed to the underlined words at the bottom of the page. "Chorionic villi sampling."

"No. You?"

"No, but I will soon."

He must have heard the sound at the exact moment

that she did, because they both turned toward the front door. A second later, Jessie heard a key sliding into the lock. She tossed the notepad back onto the table.

"This way." He caught onto her hand and hurried down the short hallway to the closet. It was tiny, she soon learned when he pushed her inside. He came in after her, squeezing the door shut.

Jessie didn't say anything, even though they were practically on top of each other. She knew how much danger they could be in. And her mind began to whirl with all the possibilities.

Had Dr. Radelman returned? Or was it one of the other kidnappers who'd followed them there? It could be just a real estate agent showing the house or a caretaker doing a routine check. After all, there were a lot of plants, and the ones left alive needed some water. But Jessie knew it wasn't that. It was too late for a routine visit from a caretaker or potential buyers.

Her heart started to pound and she felt a dizzy spell coming on. Great. Just great. Someone might come through the door to kill them, and the world whirled around the way it does when you're on a carnival ride. Because she had no choice, she closed her eyes and put her head against Jake's shoulder.

"Are you all right?" he whispered in her ear.

She tried to nod and thought maybe she had succeeded. It was hard to know—with the dizziness.

Suddenly, she could hear muffled laughter and people talking. Two people. A man and a woman.

"You're sure this is okay?" The woman giggled after her flirty sounding question.

The man made a husky growling sound. "Sure.

Like I told you, if anybody comes by, I'll just show my ID from the security company and say I was checking out the place.''

Jessie didn't allow herself to feel any relief yet, even though it didn't seem these visitors were armed and dangerous. But they were *there*. Between them and the front door. Jake probably didn't want to explain to anyone how he'd come by the key to the place.

The giggles and conversation soon turned to sounds of kissing. Then, groping. Jessie hadn't realized just how distinctive the sounds were of a couple engaged in heavy foreplay. Foreplay that was even more uncomfortable since Jake was pressed right against her.

It was pitch black in the closet. Jessie was actually thankful for that. It meant she didn't have to look at Jake's face to see how he reacted to such erotic sounds. However, she was aware, somehow, that he was looking at her.

The rhythm of his breathing changed slightly. Beneath her hand, she could feel his heart begin to pound. Muscles stirred in his chest. All of that was from the surge of adrenaline, she assured herself. That and the rather vocal couple who apparently liked to talk dirty. Hard not to react a little to that.

Too bad she couldn't move back at least an inch or two, but her back was already against the wall. However, she could do something to minimize her contact with Jake. Holding her breath, she moved her head from his shoulder. Just a fraction.

He moved at the same time. A fraction. And his mouth collided with her cheek. At first, she thought he'd tried to kiss her, but he hadn't. He put his mouth next to her ear.

"Are you okay?" he whispered. His breath brushed against her face.

No. She wasn't okay. Jessie nodded, anyway. But she really should have given that some thought first. Since Jake's mouth was still against her ear, his lips rubbed against her lobe. And the sensitive little spot just below it that she hadn't known was so sensitive.

A silent groan rumbled in her throat. She didn't make a sound, but Jessie had no doubt that he felt it. Felt it and knew what it meant. She wasn't the only one who was aware of this unexplainable attraction between them.

Slowly, a fraction at a time, he turned his head and slipped his arm around her waist. The contact was so intimate that Jessie almost panicked. Almost. Until he lowered his mouth to hers. The first touch of his lips was hardly more than a caress. But it was enough. More than enough. And after that, panicking was the absolute last thing she had on her mind.

Jake's mouth was warm and yielding. Sweet. Clever. It was all those things and more. It'd been years since a man had kissed her, and never like this. Never.

Her heartbeat slowed. Her breath became thin. The dreamy feel of pleasure seeped through her until her muscles went slack. And still he didn't stop. He continued the gentle, thorough assault. Continued to take exactly what she offered. His mouth moved over hers as if he knew every secret she'd ever hidden in her soul.

Sweet heaven, she was in a lot of trouble here.

But the kiss continued. Jake didn't deepen it. He

didn't have to. It was enough simply to have his mouth on hers. Enough for her to know this wasn't some ordinary kiss.

A slow burning hunger quickly replaced the dreamy feeling. It took Jessie a moment to realize what it was. Desire. Need. And maybe something more. But somewhere beneath the haze, beneath the fire, she knew this was wrong. She didn't trust Jake. He certainly didn't trust her. And they darn sure shouldn't complicate things with kisses. Besides, they were literally lurking in a closet. She should have her mind on plenty of other things.

Jessie eased away as much as she could. It didn't help. When she breathed, she breathed him. His taste was in her mouth. His scent covered her. Jake was the pinpointed center of all her senses, which were honed to razor-sharp edges.

In the other room, their visitors had obviously moved from foreplay to sex. She shut them out, or rather tried to. It wasn't a good idea for her to combine Jake and sex in the same thought.

"We shouldn't have done that," she whispered.

He jerked his hand from her waist and ground his forehead against hers. He cursed softly. She wanted to curse, too. And kick herself for letting this happen. She'd already made too many stupid mistakes.

"Don't move!" a man shouted.

She froze. Jake reacted with lightning speed. Somehow, he turned around, blocking her with his body. In almost the same motion, he reached down and pulled a gun from an ankle holster. She hadn't even known he was armed, but she was thankful for it.

Jessie held her breath. Died a couple of dozen

deaths. And waited out the maddening silence that followed.

The man shouted, *Don't move* again, and the lights in the living room flared on. She peeked around Jake and through the louvered slats caught a glimpse of the hulking man. In uniform. A cop.

This wasn't good. If he arrested them for trespassing, she'd have to reveal who she really was. In the long run, it might put them in even more danger. After all, if the kidnappers learned she was a former police officer, they might be especially eager to silence her. Permanently. Still, she couldn't imagine them being any more tenacious than they already were.

"What are you doing in here?" the man demanded. He hadn't said it to them, Jessie assured herself, but to the lovers.

The couple scrambled to cover themselves, both trying to answer at the same time and neither of them making much sense. "I work for the security company," the younger man said, his voice clipped. "I wanted to check out the place. My girlfriend came with me."

The cop cursed. "How long have you been here?"

"Not long." The woman, that time. Her voice shook uncontrollably. "A half-hour maybe."

"Was anybody else in here?"

The couple glanced at each other before shaking their heads. "Just us."

Another round of profanity, equally as vicious as the first. "Get the hell out!" he yelled at the couple.

Snatching up the rest of their clothes, the two hurried out the door. The cop didn't. He had his back to the closet and he kept a two-handed grip on the pistol.

Something was wrong. Very wrong. Jessie's concern turned to full-fledged fear when the man didn't move. He just stood there, his head tipped back slightly as if listening for something. Not for *something*.

For *them*.

He'd expected to find Jake and her in the house. He probably didn't have an arrest in mind, either, especially since there weren't even any handcuffs on his equipment belt.

Seconds passed. Slowly. Jessie forced herself to calm, just so he wouldn't be able to hear her breathing. God, if he turned around and saw them, they'd be trapped in the closet. And likely dead within seconds. The man's sleek, matte-black pistol would see to that.

Jake didn't move, but since she was so close to him, Jessie felt the vibration of his body. Every muscle was tense and primed, in case they had to fight their way out of this. This was the second time he'd put himself in the line of fire to protect her. At Cryogen Labs and now. She didn't like that she had to rely on anyone for safety, but she would have been terrified if Jake hadn't been there. As it was, she was just plain scared out of her mind.

The man in uniform shifted his weight slightly and eased his head higher. Another minute went by. Maybe two. He swore again and lowered his gun. She was certain he would start to search the place then, but he didn't. He left, and moments later she heard a door slam shut.

Jake pressed his fingers to her mouth as if to remind her not to say anything. Jessie needed no such reminder. They weren't out of danger yet.

"That was no cop," Jake whispered after what seemed an eternity.

"No, he wasn't. He was looking for us, Jake. I think he's one of the men who kidnapped me. And the man who fired shots at us outside Cryogen Labs."

He made a sound of agreement. "But then, how would he know we'd be here? If he followed us, he waited a long time to come inside."

That was true and it only tightened the knot in her stomach. "Who knew we were coming?" she asked. "Douglas?" It wasn't really a question. Douglas had given Jake the key. And after that warning he'd given her earlier, she definitely didn't trust him.

"He wouldn't have told anyone, but his friend who gave him the keys could have. How about you? Did you tell anyone we were coming here?"

Jessie said no right away, but it was a lie. She'd told Byron earlier when she called, but he wouldn't have said anything. Although, the phone could have been bugged.

"Douglas and I had a little talk this afternoon," she said, testing the waters. The alarmed look that Jake gave her made her even more cautious. "He believes I'll hurt your campaign."

He gritted his teeth. "I was afraid he'd say something to you. Did he scare you?"

"Not really," she lied. "It just made me wonder how much you trust him."

She obviously caught him off guard. Or something. She heard his rough intake of breath, and his gaze snapped to her.

"He's my brother-in-law."

And that didn't answer her question. "But do you trust him?"

For a moment, she thought he might laugh. Or yell. He didn't.

"Yes," Jake finally responded, although there wasn't much conviction in his voice. "Douglas is ambitious, sometimes to a fault, but Willa loves him."

It still wasn't an answer. Or maybe it was. Maybe beneath his implication of family loyalty, Jake didn't trust Douglas, either. So it meant Markham wasn't the only name on her list of suspects. She added Douglas to it.

"What now?" she asked after a long silence.

"I have some people looking for Radelman and the nurse. Beyond that, we wait. Except, from now on we're smart about it. I'm not taking any more chances with your life."

"Or yours," Jessie quickly added. "I shouldn't have brought you into this. I should have just turned it all over to the cops when I escaped from that warehouse."

Of course, in that case she would almost certainly be dead, especially since the cops hadn't believed her story. Still, if she'd wanted to, she could have convinced them by telling them the whole truth, something she wasn't especially eager to share. It wouldn't have protected her from the killers, but it might have kept Jake out of danger.

"Do I need to apologize for what just went on?" he asked.

Jessie had to look at him to make sure he was serious. Because the gunman had left the lights on, she could easily see Jake's face. He certainly seemed serious. "You don't. Do I?"

He gave an indifferent shrug. "Let's just call it a mutual lapse in judgment and leave it at that."

A lapse in judgment. Yes, that's exactly what it was. Hopefully, they had sense enough not to repeat it.

It seemed as if he was about to add more to that, but then he took a deep breath as if he'd caught a whiff of something. "Smoke," he mumbled. And then he repeated it in a much louder voice. "Damn it. He set the place on fire."

Oh God. "Let's get out of here."

Jake tore from the closet, but instead of running, he reeled toward her. "This is probably a trap."

Her throat snapped shut and she nodded. Yes, it was a trap—that should have occurred to her right away. "He'll be expecting us to go out the back."

"Then, we'll have to leave through the front. Stay behind me. And I mean it." Jake latched on to her arm and rushed to the front door. On the way there, he yanked a tiny phone from his pocket and called 911. He said nothing more than their address and that there was a fire.

He put the phone away and turned the knob, but when he pulled, the door didn't budge. He gave it a fierce shake. "It's blocked. Someone really wants us dead."

Smoke started to float through the room, and Jessie didn't think it was her imagination that it was already getting hotter. "We'll go out the window."

With Jake leading the way, they hurried to the large corner window. One glance, however, and he cursed. Jessie didn't have to ask why. She saw the lock. Jake frantically riffled through his pocket for the key Douglas had given him.

"Hurry," she said under her breath.

She could feel the flames already eating their way through to the interior of the house. Jake rammed the key into the lock. But it merely glanced off. He tried again, adding a mumbled mixture of prayers and threats, but it was obvious that it wasn't the right key.

"Breaking the glass won't help," he said.

It wouldn't. Thick metal casings held in each small pane. Even if they broke the glass, the space wouldn't be large enough for them to escape. A security measure, no doubt. And a death trap for them.

Black smoke oozed through the front door. On the porch, there was already a thick orangy wall of flames. They wouldn't get through that now. And where was the fire department? Jessie wasn't sure if it'd been merely seconds or minutes since Jake made that call.

He caught her by the hand again and hurried down the hall to the bedrooms. Both had windows with the same tiny panes. And locks. By the time they made it back out into the living room, the smoke was thick and black.

"On the floor," Jake instructed.

The lights went out, plunging the room into darkness. Jake immediately turned on his flashlight and held it in his mouth. He pulled her down next to him, and on their hands and knees they crawled toward the kitchen.

Jessie's muscles felt heavy and her lungs began to ache. She wouldn't let herself think about what this might do to the baby, but raw rage shot through her.

She *wouldn't* die—because it would mean her baby would die. Somehow, they would have to get out alive.

When they reached the back door, he put the still-lit flashlight into his pocket and shoved the gun into her hand. "You think you can use that if you have to?"

"Yes." Without blinking an eye. But she didn't understand why he'd given it to her. At least, she didn't understand until she saw him reach for the knob. It turned in his hand. So it wasn't blocked.

"What do you think you're doing?" she demanded.

"I'm going out there, and you'll be right behind me."

All the smoke and the shortness of breath made it hard for her to think straight, but it didn't take her long to figure out that this was a really stupid plan. "Whoever is out there will shoot you."

He shrugged. "Then you'll drop to the ground and shoot them."

Jessie couldn't believe what she'd just heard. "Well, that doesn't sound like much of a deal for you. I can't let you do this."

"Yes, you can. For the baby."

That was dirty pool. Jessie groaned. Coughed. And tried to argue. But she couldn't. This wasn't about her, not really. He was offering her baby a chance to live.

Maybe.

And maybe the gunman would just shoot them both when they went out that back door.

"A different scenario," she insisted. "We go through the door together. We go out low and hit the

ground or the porch, or whatever's out there. Then I
shoot at the first thing that moves.''

''No deal.''

She knew from his pigheaded, resolute tone that
he meant it. Mercy, why did he have to be so stubborn?

A swirl of smoke billowed around her face and
Jessie choked back a cough. This certainly wasn't the
time to contemplate every aspect of a plan that had
little or no chance of being successful, anyway.

She shoved the gun back into his hand. ''All right.
Do your Boy Scout thing, but be careful.''

It seemed such a paltry way to send him out on
what could easily be a suicide mission. He didn't
help matters when he brushed a kiss on her forehead.

He turned the knob and in the same motion shoved
his shoulder against the door. It flew open. No
flames, thank God. The fresh air rushed at them. Both
gulped in deep breaths. Jake clotheslined his arm
across her chest and peered out into the darkness.
Jessie did some peering of her own.

Nothing.

At least, nothing she could see. But then, a gunman wouldn't likely stand out in the open because
the fire had possibly already attracted witnesses.
He'd no doubt taken cover. Or else was long gone.
She could only pray that he'd left the scene.

In the distance the sirens howled. Jake didn't wait
for them to get closer. He couldn't. The fire crackled
and hissed behind them. Crouching, he made his way
onto the porch, with her following.

They paused a moment at the steps that led into
the yard. Jessie figured if someone planned to shoot

at them, it would be a perfect time to do it. But there were no shots.

"We're getting out of here," Jake muttered.

She had no plans to disagree. He latched on to her hand and broke into a run. And they didn't stop until they were blocks away from the burning house.

Chapter Nine

Dr. Lisette opened the door to Jessie's bedroom and motioned for Jake to come inside. "We're all done."

Jake entered slowly, his gaze immediately searching for Jessie. She was in the chair next to the bed. Other than looking a little nervous, she seemed all right.

"Jessie said it was okay if you were here while we talked," the doctor explained.

Jake would tell her later how much he appreciated that. She could have shut him out and he wouldn't have blamed her. After all, he still hadn't admitted to her that this was his child. He hadn't even cut her any slack. But then, with the exception of this, she hadn't given him many breaks, either.

"How's Jessie doing?" Jake asked. "Did the smoke from the fire, uh, hurt her in any way?"

"Not that I can tell. I drew some blood and I'll send it to the lab just to make sure. I think Jessie's about ten weeks along in the pregnancy." He turned to her. "Does that match with the date you think you were inseminated?"

She nodded and glanced at Jake. She didn't hold the gaze long before she looked away.

"So I'm estimating a January due date," Dr. Lisette continued, when no one else said anything. "I have a colleague, an obstetrician, that I'd like to refer you to. He'll no doubt want to schedule you for an ultrasound as well as a complete physical."

Jake didn't like the sound of that. "Do you think something is wrong with the baby?"

"No. It's just routine. An obstetrician would probably want to do an ultrasound even if this baby had been conceived the usual way."

Jessie cleared her throat. "What about a DNA test? How soon could one of those be done?"

Dr. Lisette picked up his bag. "As early as nine weeks, but I suspect you've already had one administered. There appears to be a needle mark on your lower abdomen."

"Yes," she said softly. "They did some kind of test. I don't know what. Before they did it, they made me drink a reddish-colored liquid. An antihistamine, the woman said. In fact, they gave me that a lot of times." She paused, her breath catching in her throat. "Would that affect the baby?"

The doctor shook his head. "Not likely. The test, though—that does carry some risks. A small percentage of the women who have this procedure miscarry."

The color drained from Jessie's face. Jake knew the feeling. There were already enough risks to this baby without adding more.

"Then, she won't have the test," Jake insisted.

The doctor's thick eyebrows quirked. "Well, it's possible we could get the results from the one she's already had. Do you know the name of the lab they used?"

Jessie shook her head. "I have no idea."

"Well, I'll make some calls and see if I can find out anything. We might get lucky." Dr. Lisette started for the door. "In the meantime, fill that prescription for the vitamins. Exercise regularly. Eat right. In other words, do the things you're supposed to do, anyway." He stopped and glanced at Jake before returning his gaze to Jessie. "You don't have to limit your sexual activity, either. That's something people usually want to know."

Because Jake still had his attention on Jessie, he saw her startled expression. "Thank you for coming," Jake told the doctor. "Just send me the bill for this."

"Ms. Barrett already paid me, in cash. She insisted." And with that, Dr. Lisette left.

Jake frowned. Sheesh, the woman was stubborn. He was the one who demanded that she have the exam and he was more than willing to pay for it.

Jessie popped up out of the chair and walked to the balcony doors. "I didn't ask him about having sex. He brought that up on his own."

"I didn't think you would say anything about it to him. Perhaps that's why Dr. Lisette mentioned it. Maybe he thought he was doing us a favor or something."

She laughed, short and crisp. "He has no idea, does he." Apparently not expecting an answer, Jessie stared out the glass doors. "Why didn't you insist I have that DNA test?"

"The risk of miscarriage." And because it wouldn't prove anything he didn't already know.

So why didn't he just tell Jessie that?

Jake shook his head. He still didn't trust her, that's

why. With reason. She might be the very one out to ruin him.

"But it might have proven the father of this child," Jessie pointed out.

The father. Jessie had been careful not to name him again. Maybe she was tired of his denial. He certainly was. Still, the denial, even unspoken, was all he could offer her right now.

"There's a safer way to do that. We can wait until the baby's born and do the test then."

"That won't be for nearly seven months. Maybe longer, since they might not want to do a test on a newborn. You're willing to wait until then?"

"Are you?" he fired back.

She didn't look at him when she spoke. "The test doesn't matter to me. I've been examined and prodded enough to last a lifetime." Jessie took a deep breath and folded her arms over her chest. "Listen, in a day or two I'll be leaving, anyway. I'll—"

"Wait a minute. You don't even know who's trying to kill you. How can you possibly think of leaving while you're in danger?"

"I might never find out who's behind this. I can't hang around waiting for the worst to happen. But I'll keep in touch with you. That is, if you want me to."

Jake couldn't believe what he'd heard. "If I want you to?" Of course, he wanted her to. Damn it, this was his child.

"For the DNA test," she clarified. "I'll try to have one done as soon as the baby comes. I'll call you and let you know the results."

"You'll call me," he flatly repeated. And while she was at it, she might let him know if he had a son or a daughter. No. It wouldn't work that way. It wouldn't. "I can arrange a place for you to stay. A place with security. You'd have proper medical supervision."

She turned toward him, a cynical smile on her face. "You're doing that Boy Scout thing again. It's not necessary, you know. I've been taking care of myself since I was sixteen. In a day or two, I have to leave."

Jake locked his jaw to keep himself from telling her what she could do with that suggestion. She was cutting him out. Or trying to. It wouldn't work. He wouldn't let it work. If she left, it was possible he'd never find her again.

And worse, the killer might.

Jessie was wrong—taking care of her was necessary. That meant becoming a part of her life as well as the baby's.

"Please," he said, speaking as calmly as he could manage. "I want you to stay until we're sure you're safe."

She paused and combed her suddenly concerned gaze over his face. "Something's wrong. You aren't treating me the way you were yesterday."

Had he been that obvious? Apparently. "What am I doing that's different?" He'd try to fix it right away. He didn't want to tell her his suspicions about the baby. Not yet. No need to bare his heart to a woman capable of stomping it into the ground. Besides, maybe he was wrong.

Except, he knew he wasn't.

Jessie ran her fingers through her hair. The little maneuver also hiked up her waist-length top. Jake caught a glimpse of bare skin, of her navel, and he didn't have to look hard for them, either. "You're being nice to me," she explained. "Too nice."

Was he? It was difficult to be heartless to the woman carrying his child. A child he had thought he would never have. Still, Jake wouldn't let himself think beyond that. Things weren't settled by a long shot.

"Hey, what can I say?" He forced some cockiness into his tone. "I'm a nice guy."

Jessie just stood there, her hand in her hair and her navel visible. "Yes, you are."

Jake couldn't have been more shocked if she'd hit him. He couldn't even talk. Couldn't move.

"Do me a favor, though. Don't be nice too often, okay?" Jessie didn't look at him when she continued. "I'm not myself these days. I mean, I don't usually let people get to me, and you're getting to me with all this nice-guy stuff."

Okay. On some level he understood that. She was getting to him, as well. He just didn't know what to do about it. "So you don't want me to be nice?"

"Not *that* nice."

Jake went to her, put his fingers under her chin, lifting it slightly so they made eye contact. "All right, stay here and quit giving me your sass."

"Sass?" Her eyebrow rose.

"All right. Bad choice of words." He added some gruffness to his voice. "Don't give me any of your usual crap."

Jessie gave a lopsided smile. "Much better."

"Now it's your turn. Say something snippy and give me one of those go-to-the-netherworld looks. You know which one I mean. It's where your mouth is in a flat line and your eyes are narrowed."

She complied. But it quickly faded. "Mercy, this is crazy. I have enough to worry about without adding you to the list, Jake. Tell me you can take care of yourself."

"I can take care of myself," he assured her. And her, as well.

She slowly lifted her gaze. Gone was the teasing expression and pretense of confidence. There was a lot of concern swirling in her silver-gray eyes. Jake didn't know how to react to that concern. He didn't dare let himself feel good about it.

"All this worry is only natural, Jessie." At least, he hoped like the devil it was. "We're in the middle of this, whatever it is, together. That creates a sort of warped camaraderie."

"Yes," she said softly. She blew out a long breath and some of the tension faded from her eyes. "That's all there is to it. Good."

She didn't clarify that last remark, and Jake didn't want it clarified. He was about to tell her goodbye, but Jessie spoke first.

"I don't usually admit this, but I'm scared. I mean, I'm used to watching out for myself, but it's like I'm not just myself anymore. There's this whole other person and I'm responsible for it." She shook her head. "For him, or her. Anyway, if something bad happens—"

"It won't."

She continued as if she hadn't even heard him. "If it does, make sure you get the person behind this. I don't want anyone walking, if they do something to hurt this child."

Oh, they would pay all right, if the worst happened. But he had no intention of letting it get to that point. He'd do everything within his power to keep Jessie safe. The baby raised the stakes to the highest level.

Jake slid his hand down her arm. A gentle caress that she apparently needed as much as he did. "You don't have to be scared, Jessie."

He was scared enough for both of them.

JESSIE THOUGHT she would get a moment to herself, but when Jake opened the door to leave, Willa was standing there, both hands filled with huge shopping bags.

"Jake said you needed clothes," Willa said none too enthusiastically. She turned her equally unenthusiastic gaze to her brother. "Douglas is downstairs. He says it's important that he speak to you in private. I warn you, though, he's in a snit about something."

Great. Jessie knew what that meant. She'd get left alone with Willa, a woman who obviously detested her.

"You'll be okay, Jessie?" Jake asked.

She wanted to say no, but she couldn't keep tearing him away from his business and the campaign. Jessie nodded finally, and Willa gave him a gentle nudge into the hallway. Within seconds of his departure, she deposited the bags on the bed and shut the door.

The woman put her hands on her slender hips and matched Jessie's frown. "Okay, let me save us some time and just ask this outright. Did Douglas come on to you?"

Of all the things Jessie had imagined she might say, that wasn't one of them. "No."

Willa leaned closer and gave her a considering

look. After a moment, she simply nodded. "He said he didn't, but he's lied through his teeth before. I just wanted to make sure."

Jessie just stared at her. Willa had no icy facade today and her laser-blue eyes were rimmed red as if she'd spent hours crying. Apparently crying over some advances she thought Douglas had made. There'd been no advances. Far from it. He'd threatened Jessie.

"Good grief." Willa covered her face with her hands. "Maybe Douglas is right. Maybe I am losing my mind."

Jessie wasn't about to agree with her. Besides, maybe Willa had good reason to suspect her husband of fooling around.

Willa eased her hands back down. "All right, I've already made a complete fool of myself, so I might as well go for broke. What kind of spell did you put on my brother?"

"Wonderful," Jessie mumbled under her breath. Part two of the conversation she didn't want to have. "Look, let me save you some trouble. I'm not in the same league as the McClendons or Anne, and I know that doesn't please you. But I'll be out of Jake's life soon." Jessie started toward the door, but Willa stepped in front of her.

"You'll break his heart," Willa insisted. "That's what I'm trying to stop. I don't want to see Jake get hurt."

Jessie almost laughed at the notion of breaking Jake's heart. He'd have to care about her for that to happen, and he didn't. Well, he didn't care beyond trying to get to the bottom of how her predicament might affect him. Heck, he'd even called those kisses in the closet a *lapse in judgment.* Hardly the words of a man on the verge of a broken heart.

"Anne's death nearly destroyed him," Willa added, obviously not ready to let the subject drop. "She died in childbirth. Did you know that?"

Jessie felt her composure slip a considerable notch. "No."

"Anne didn't want children. Jake did. So after he was fairly sure he'd won his battle with Hodgkin's Disease, he talked her into getting pregnant."

Jessie started to walk away again, but that stopped her. He'd talked his wife into getting pregnant. And she had died trying to give birth to that child.

"He blames himself," Jessie muttered uneasily.

"You bet he does. And before this campaign, he'd lost the will to live. There are days I actually thank God for Abel Markham. If Jake hadn't wanted to keep the man out of office, he might never have gotten over Anne's death."

"But now he has, and you're scared I'll mess things up."

Willa moved even closer, until they were only inches apart. "I'm scared because I don't want him rushing into anything that could cause him more pain."

Jessie started to give Willa another assurance, but then she caught the scent of Willa's perfume. She didn't know the name of the expensive scent, but Jessie definitely recognized it. From that night. The night the three people kidnapped her. Jessie was sure someone had worn the same perfume.

"Are you all right?" Willa asked.

"Fine," she managed to say. She couldn't let her imagination run wild on this. After all, a lot of women probably wore that scent. And as much as she distrusted coincidences, this could easily be one.

Willa took her by the arm and led her to the chair by the balcony door. "Sit down. Jake will have my head if he finds out I've upset you."

Jessie pushed her hair away from her face. "I'm not upset."

"I don't believe that. Look, I didn't mean to insult you. I guess I never learned how to keep my mouth shut." She sank onto the edge of the bed.

Jessie almost let that remark pass, but then decided to put it to the test. Just how much would Willa tell her? "I've been thinking about Markham's visit."

"Hmm." Willa certainly didn't look alarmed by the comment. She reached into one of the bags and began to pull out some of the items. "What about it?"

Jessie idly looked at the dress and the underwear that Willa laid out on the bed. Her mind definitely wasn't on clothes. "He said something about a woman's body found on the property."

"Christy Mendoza," Willa provided. "Markham's tried to use her death to sling mud at Jake."

"Is there any mud to sling?"

Willa froze and snared Jessie's gaze. "Please don't tell me you think Jake had something to do with that."

"No. I just wanted to know if Markham can make it seem as if Jake did."

"Jake didn't even know Ms. Mendoza. She came to the barbecue because she worked for the caterer. The only time I saw her was when Douglas was following her around. She brushed him off."

Willa must have noticed Jessie's questioning

glance because she added, "More than one person gleefully told me that. When you have a cheating husband, people just love to remind you of it every chance they get."

Jessie didn't doubt it. She didn't even doubt that Christy had refused Douglas's advances. Christy might have had no inhibitions about working in a skimpy, show-all outfit, but she wouldn't have fooled around with a married man. It did make Jessie wonder, though, how Douglas had reacted to Christy's rejection. For that matter, how had Willa felt about her husband's behavior that night? It was something to consider.

From the statements Jessie had read, there were at least two hundred guests at that party. Technically, any one of them could have killed Christy and set it up to look like an accident. After all, Christy was petite, barely five feet tall. She couldn't have put up much of a fight, especially if she hadn't perceived the person to be a threat.

Jessie tried to block out that image. Her friend, a woman she loved, fighting for her life. It was that image, that nightmare, that kept her awake plenty of times. The only trauma to the body had been a blow to the back of the head. It was an injury consistent with someone slipping on a rock, but Jessie had never been able to accept that Christy would be that careless. Besides, Christy wasn't the sort for a solo walk in the moonlight.

Now Jessie had to figure out if Christy's death was connected to the rest of what happened. Was it connected to her? Right from the start, she'd downplayed that idea, but maybe it was time to reconsider it. After all, both Willa and Douglas were connected to Christy, and they were indirectly connected to Jessie.

"So what do you think of this dress?" she heard Willa ask.

Jessie was about to say something polite, when she realized that feigned politeness wasn't necessary. The dress was a simple cut and the color of ripe peaches. It was beautiful. "Thanks. I just hope I can afford it."

"You can. Jake's paying for it." Willa added a not-so-subtle sigh to that.

"No, he's not," Jessie quickly assured her. "I'll pay him back every cent."

That only seemed to amuse Willa. "By the way, when you tell Jake about our little talk, be kind," she said, standing. "He won't appreciate my interference. He never does. That's why I've found these little behind-the-back sessions necessary."

The callously offered remark caught Jessie off guard. Hard to do, since she'd braced herself for just about anything. It made her wonder how many more behind-the-back sessions Willa had orchestrated. And just what lengths would she go to to protect her brother?

Jessie managed to tell her goodbye. Willa did the same and, moving with a graceful stride, left the room.

She pressed her fingers to her temples to try to soothe away the headache that was just starting to brew. Everything was so mixed up. Jessie could blame herself for that. It was stupid, but she had allowed herself to become involved with a man that she had only days earlier suspected of murder. Some cop she'd turned out to be.

Doing what she should have done days earlier, she mentally walked herself back through the evidence, adding the bits and pieces she'd learned from Jake, Willa, Douglas and even Markham. It was all still a confusing puzzle. Markham might be the one behind the insemination plot, but he hadn't killed Christy. He wasn't even at the party. So maybe the two things weren't connected.

Of course, that left one glaring question—who wanted her dead? Markham, maybe, if for some reason he suddenly wanted to put a stop to a plot he'd set into motion. Or maybe the person trying to kill her was Douglas. After all, Douglas had known Jake and she were going to Radelman's. Douglas also had a motive, if she factored in the trust fund. And if he'd somehow found out about the baby.... That wouldn't have been so difficult. She'd left the home pregnancy test sitting in her motel room. Douglas could have followed Jake and gone into the room after they left. He could have seen the test results, put two and two together, and figured she was a threat to Willa's half of the trust fund.

But then, Willa had the same motive.

Jessie groaned. The puzzle still had too many pieces, especially with Dr. Radelman, Marion Cameron and the two guards still on the loose.

Knowing she needed to check in, she went to the phone and dialed Byron's number. As usual, he picked up right away.

"I just wanted to make sure the money will be there tomorrow," she said, after they got past the greetings.

"Sure, but give me until three o'clock. I want to deliver it to you in person."

"You can't," she insisted. "You've done enough for me already." Maybe too much. Jessie hated to ask the next question, but she had to know if Byron accidentally leaked the fact that she had gone to Radelman's house. "Listen, by any chance have you mentioned to anyone that you've talked to me?"

"No, of course not. Why?"

She ignored that for the time being. "Could anyone have overheard our conversations?"

"No, I was careful. What's this all about, Jess?"

"I'm not sure, but don't trust anyone, okay?"

"I won't if you won't," he quickly answered.

"Don't worry, I don't intend to trust anyone until I find out what's really going on around here."

"Does that include McClendon?"

Did it? It had to, even though her heart whispered differently. "Yes, that includes Jake. Take care, Byron."

She hung up, turned around and saw Jake in the doorway. She quickly replayed the conversation in her head and knew there was no good way for him to interpret that last part.

"A friend?" he questioned, his eyes narrowed almost to straight slits.

"Yes." Because she suddenly didn't know what to do with her hands, she pushed them through her hair. "I thought you were with Douglas."

His expression didn't relax much. "We're finished, and he and Willa are ready to leave for a meeting. I need to go with them." He paused. "By the way, I told Douglas everything."

She nodded. That made sense. Well, it made sense only because Jake didn't consider him a suspect. It still didn't change her opinion of his brother-in-law.

"Douglas found out something from the police," Jake added. "And I wanted to tell you before you heard it on the news."

That didn't do anything to steady her rattled nerves. "What?"

"They found Dr. Radelman's body earlier."

Oh God. Jessie had known they would. There was no way the doctor's boss would have left him alive so he could go to the police. Still, a chill went through her. It was a brutal reminder of what this person wanted to do to her.

"He was murdered?"

Jake shook his head. "Seems he lost control of his car and went off a bridge over in Kendall County."

"It was no accident," she whispered.

"No." He didn't move from the doorway. Jake just stood there and pushed out a long breath. "Listen, I need to go. You'll be all right?"

"Sure." It was a lie, but there was nothing he could do to give her peace of mind.

For her, peace of mind didn't exist anymore.

Chapter Ten

It was almost dark before Jake arrived back at the ranch. And he'd seethed the whole afternoon. Only one thing had been on his mind—Jessie. The tail end of the conversation he heard was all the proof he needed that she was still lying to him.

Hell, how had he let himself even begin to trust her? Yet it had happened. Not only had he started to trust her, he'd kissed her, for Christ's sake! Kissed her and allowed himself to care about her. And in doing so, she had sucked him right into her web of lies.

He went through the house, searching, until he found her on the balcony outside her bedroom. "We need to talk." He didn't wait for her to ask, *about what?* and he didn't even try to contain the anger in his voice. "I want to know what you're keeping from me."

She flexed her eyebrows and almost calmly turned her gaze back to the scenery. "For a politician, you don't beat around the bush."

"It wastes time. So who was it on the phone earlier—a boyfriend?"

Jessie gave him a lopsided smile. "A friend friend."

And perhaps a boyfriend. Jake wouldn't discount it just on her denial. "He knows about the kidnapping?"

She nodded.

"The pregnancy?"

"I told him, yes."

He had to hesitate a moment and get control of the punch he had just felt in his gut. "And you trust him?"

"I've known him a long time. He's like a brother."

A brother and a friend. A guy close enough to have Jessie's complete confidence. He caught her shoulder, turning her so she faced him. "Did you tell him we were going to Radelman's house?"

"Yes, but—"

"No buts," Jake snapped. "Someone sent that fake cop to find us. It could have been this friend that you trust."

Her mouth dropped open. "And it easily could have been your own brother-in-law, since he's the one who came up with the key. Have you asked Douglas if he told anyone?"

"As a matter of fact, I did. He said he didn't tell a soul."

"Well, gee, now I feel a whole lot better. He knew about it and he could have told anyone, including his wife." She shook off his grip and headed back to her room.

Jake followed her inside, catching up with her before she could shut the balcony door in his face. He wouldn't let her get away that easily. "Care to explain that."

She reeled toward him, some fire slashing through her gray eyes. "I smelled perfume the night they kidnapped me. It's the same scent your sister wears."

Now she was accusing Willa? "And that proves what, exactly? We'd already figured the woman was probably Marion Cameron, the nurse from Cryogen Labs. It's not much of a stretch for us to assume she could have worn perfume. Unless you're saying there were two women there—the nurse and my sister."

Jessie blew out a long breath, and the fire in her eyes turned to frustration. "No. There was only one woman, but we have no idea who's pulling the strings behind the scenes, do we?"

"Okay, I'll bite," Jake said, giving that some thought. "What would my sister's motive be?"

"I don't know. Maybe money?"

"Just how would that connect to you? To your kidnapping? If Willa's motivation is money, then she wouldn't take shots at me. In my will, I've left everything to my late wife's memorial fund. If I'm dead, my sister doesn't collect a cent."

Jessie quickly came up with something else. "Then, maybe the trust fund. Douglas mentioned that."

He stepped closer. "Not that, either. If Willa was after the trust fund, then the last thing she'd want is you carrying my baby."

Jessie grumbled under her breath. "You're right. Because then neither of you would inherit it. The child would."

"And even the child's mother couldn't get her

hands on it," Jake calmly added. "But maybe you didn't know that."

There was nothing calm about the emotion that swept through Jessie's voice. "So you're back to accusing me. Sweet heaven, if you really think I'm capable of that, then why not just kick me out?" Her gaze darted around the room and landed on her purse. She quickly snatched it up. "On second thought, I'll kick myself out. I've had enough of this so-called protection of yours. I've never felt more unsafe in my life."

She nearly made it to the door, before he latched on to her arm. It didn't stop her. Jessie tried to sling him off, first by twisting her body and then by shoving her elbow into his stomach. It wasn't a gentle shove, either. Jake sputtered out a cough, but somehow managed to hold on to her arm.

"Let go of me!" She jerked toward the door, but her fingers only glanced off the knob.

"Not until you listen."

"I have listened and I'm tired of hearing what you have to say."

Jake managed to catch her other arm before she could wallop him with her purse. He pinned her hands to the back of the door. It wasn't the best position. His body was now squashed against hers. He'd fantasized about getting her into his arms, but certainly not like this.

"I'm sorry," he managed to say, just before she elbowed him again in the stomach. Jake rattled out another cough. Jesus. The woman fought like a wildcat.

She either didn't hear what he said or she didn't believe him. They both grappled for position and his body pressed into hers to keep her from getting away again. Somehow their gazes met, coming together to a screeching halt. Her gray eyes were wide. Startled. And her breath raced wild and hot.

"I'm sorry," he repeated.

She stilled immediately, blinked, and he felt her muscles go limp. Jake had to catch her in his arms to keep her from sagging to the floor. A sob tore from her mouth. Then another, before Jessie buried her face against his shoulder.

"I can't cry," she mumbled. "I hate to cry."

He didn't doubt it. And Jake felt like a jackass. He'd actually wrestled with a pregnant woman, pinned her to the door, and then made her cry.

"It's all right," he whispered. He didn't know what else to say to her. Or to do. There weren't many things that could make him feel as miserable as hearing Jessie cry.

"No. It's not. Crying won't make it better. It never makes anything better."

But the sobs continued. Jake scooped her up in his arms and sat on the bed. She didn't resist when he started to stroke her hair.

"I don't want your damn money," she mumbled. "Or that trust fund. I don't want anything from you."

"I know." And he did know that, deep in his heart. This was a woman who wouldn't let him buy her a cheeseburger. She had even paid for the physical that he'd arranged.

Without releasing his grip on her, he leaned back to rest against the headboard. Jake glanced at her out of the corner of his eye. And his gaze soon fell on the short white skirt she wore. And her legs. Unfortunately, that was just the beginning of the little journey that his gaze made. He gave her a thorough once-over before he got to her face. At that point, he realized that if he had any sense, he'd get up right now and take a cold shower.

He apparently didn't have any sense.

He stayed put.

She ran her finger over her eyebrow. The gesture seemed oddly provocative to him. Of course, with the way he was feeling, anything would have seemed provocative.

"Boy, I just made a fool of myself, didn't I," she said softly.

"No. You just cried, that's all."

"Sheesh." She sniffed and wiped the tears off her cheeks with the back of her hand. "This hormone stuff is worse than PMS."

"You've had your life turned upside down. You're allowed to cry after everything you've been through."

"Maybe. But I've never been fond of people who boo-hoo all over the place." She rolled out of his embrace, landing on the mattress beside him. "I'll try not to do it again."

"I'm the one who needs to say I'm sorry. I had no right to accuse you of trying to get that trust fund."

She turned her head toward him and frowned. "You're being nice again. I'd rather you didn't do that right now."

He shifted on the bed, rolling on his side. "I have to be nice. It might make up for what I just did. I didn't hurt you, did I?"

Jessie chuckled, but the sound was filled with

nerves. "No, but I'll bet you have sore ribs. Sorry about elbowing you."

"I deserved it. It's just that when I heard you on the phone with your friend—"

"And he's just that," she interrupted. "I felt like I needed to tell someone before I lost my mind."

He couldn't help but notice the slight tremble of her bottom lip. It wasn't a good thing for him to notice. It reminded him of how vulnerable she must feel. Of how vulnerable she was. It reminded him of other things, too. It reminded him of her mouth.

Before he could talk himself out of it, Jake leaned over her. Closer to her.

Immediately, there was a startled look in her eyes. "What do you think you're doing?"

A good question. Too bad he didn't have a good answer. "I'm muddying the waters." Jake dipped his head lower, intending to kiss her. He changed his mind on the way down and brushed his mouth against her earlobe. Jessie shivered, a tiny sound coming from deep within her throat.

All right. Since he'd already done something insane and since she seemed to enjoy it, there seemed to be no way to stop him. This time he nuzzled the little area just below her ear, dampened it slightly with the tip of his tongue and then blew his breath over the same spot.

Jessie whimpered.

Another *all right.* She responded the way his body wanted her to respond. Obviously disgusted with him, his brain had apparently already shut itself off.

Jake went from her ear to her cheek, making the journey one long, slow kiss. She tasted good. Like something forbidden. Like something necessary.

Like Jessie.

He suddenly needed her mouth and took it, twisting and knotting his fingers through her hair so he completely controlled the movement of her head. The overly soft mattress shifted, easing him farther over, until he was nearly on top of her. Jessie didn't resist him. Just the opposite. She wrapped her arms around him and pulled him even closer. Apparently she intended to muddy some waters, as well.

"Is this uncomfortable for you?" he asked. He was practically on top of her. A place he darn sure shouldn't be, especially considering his body was now as hard as granite. She seemed so small. Fragile.

And *his*.

But she wasn't his by a long shot.

Her voice was soft and feathery. Hardly any substance. The voice of an aroused woman. "I wish it were uncomfortable."

His eyebrow rose.

"If it were," she explained. "Then, I could ask you to move."

So Jessie wouldn't give him an out. If there was to be an out, it would have to come from him. Jake was about a hundred percent sure he wouldn't stop. He proved that to himself when he kissed her again and reached for her top.

The loose fabric didn't give him much resistance, either, when he caught the scooped neck and eased it down. No bra. He knew there wouldn't be. There was only woman beneath, and he lowered the top until he could see her breasts. Creamy white. Small and well shaped. Perfect.

He met her gaze and saw his need mirrored in her shimmering gray eyes. Jake used his tongue to wet his fingertips and slipped them over her nipples. Pleasing her. Pleasing himself.

Her mouth opened. Her hips arched slightly, seeking him, but he dodged what would have been a well-placed nudge. He couldn't have her do that, yet. His restraint would go to hell in a handbasket if she touched him that way.

"This is really crazy," she whispered.

You bet it was. As crazy as it got. He was doing some heavy foreplay with a woman he shouldn't be playing with. Of course, his body didn't care about that. Jake figured in a minute or two, he wouldn't care, either. He wanted her breasts. In his mouth. And he didn't want to stop there.

Jake lowered his head and brushed the tip of his tongue over one of her dusky rose-colored nipples. Her eyes glazed over, and her back bowed, thrusting her breasts higher so he could easily take her nipple into his mouth.

He did.

When his lips closed around the hard bud and his tongue circled it, drawing it deeply into his mouth, she bucked beneath him. He wasn't able to dodge her this time. The woman was good. She managed to locate the hardest part of his body with the softest part of hers. It was like striking a match. There was heat. Fire. Jake hissed through his teeth and looked down at her.

"You're making me crazy," she mumbled.

Yes, and she was returning the favor.

Jessie caught his arm when he slid lower and kissed her stomach. Somehow, he managed to focus so he could see her eyes. Her beautiful gray eyes. She didn't say anything, but he could see the struggle going on inside her head. Jake struggled too, but this need, these feelings that gnawed away at him over-powered any doubts.

Since his heartbeat was drumming in his ears, at first he thought he was hearing things. When Jessie's eyes widened, he knew that he wasn't. Someone was pounding on the door.

"Who is it?" Jake called out.

"It's Ellen. Sorry to disturb you, but Ms. Barrett has a visitor. Detective DuCiel from Austin PD. One of the ranch hands was at the gate and let him in when he showed his badge. He's in the living room and says he needs to speak to Ms. Barrett right away."

Jake didn't like the sound of that. But then, ap-parently neither did Jessie. Mumbling profanity un-der her breath, she barreled off the bed and began to fix her clothes.

Chapter Eleven

Jessie's mouth tightened until she felt her jaw muscles cramp. "Byron is here?" she mumbled. Whatever could the man be thinking, coming to the house with Jake around?

Jake gave her a puzzled look. Jessie was sure he didn't look any more puzzled than she did, and it wasn't just from that steamy kissing session. "Byron from the phone call?" he asked.

"Yes."

"He's a cop?"

She heard the surprise in Jake's voice. It no doubt matched the aggravation in hers. "Yes." And perhaps he'd soon be a cop with a wrung neck.

Jessie checked herself in the mirror. She looked as if she'd just been ravaged. She glanced at Jake—he looked ravaged, as well. Hopefully, Byron wouldn't notice that. "You might want to tuck in your shirt."

Jake did and ran his hand through his hair to straighten it. "I thought you didn't trust cops."

She didn't answer him. Jessie headed out of the bedroom and downstairs. Jake trailed right behind her. Not that she thought he would let her go alone. After all, he didn't know Byron, and the fact he'd learned her friend was a cop probably piqued his interest.

They went through the archway into the living room, Jessie already bracing herself for an argument. However, the first thing she saw was the gun. And Byron aimed it right at Jake.

Jessie gasped. "What the—"

"Move away from him, Jess!" Byron ordered.

"Have you lost your mind?" She caught Jake's arm when he tried to step in front of her. He mumbled something steeped with anger. "This isn't what you think," she assured Jake. "My friend is obviously not thinking straight."

Byron didn't lower the gun, even when Jessie took a step toward him. "Oh, I'm not the one with problems with reality," he insisted. "Jake McClendon has brainwashed you."

If she hadn't been so scared that the situation might escalate, she would have laughed. Jessie took another step toward Byron. Or at least tried to.

Jake caught her and pulled her back. He directed his comments, however, at Byron. "I don't care if you're a cop or not, get that gun out of my face."

"Yes," Jessie agreed through clenched teeth.

But Byron kept the gun aimed. Jessie had never seen him like this, his expression a tight mask of raw emotion. Obviously, her situation had pushed him over the edge. She hoped it was not so far that he would do something stupid.

"Are you the one who had Jessie kidnapped?" Jake demanded.

Jessie groaned again. She started to reassure him that Byron couldn't do anything like that. The reassurance, though, stuck in her throat when she glanced at the gun again. She quickly pushed aside the feelings of betrayal and fear. Byron wouldn't betray her. The only reason she had that shiver down the back of her neck was that he had his weapon drawn.

Still...

"Put that gun away, Byron," she insisted. "You're scaring me."

That seemed to work. Byron swept his gaze from her to Jake and then back again. A moment later and while mumbling to himself, he lowered the gun and eased it back into the shoulder holster beneath his jacket.

"Give me a good reason why I shouldn't grab you by the scruff of your neck and throw you out of my house." Jake didn't yell. He kept his voice low and dangerous.

Jessie successfully managed to step between them. "Because Byron is going to behave himself, or else I'll grab him by the scruff and throw him out." She crossed the room and got in his face. "What the heck is wrong with you?" she whispered.

He didn't answer. Jake didn't say anything else, either. That's because they were in the process of sizing each other up. It was a real study in contrasts. Jake was dressed casually—jeans, boots and a leather vest that was the same color as his chocolate-brown hair. Byron, as usual, was groomed to a T in an Italian suit he couldn't afford and was probably still paying off on his credit card.

Jake's scowl didn't fade any. "Jessie tells me you're a friend?" It was definitely a question—one with other questions attached. Was Byron really a friend or was he her lover? And just what the heck was he doing here?

"Jess and I go way back," Byron said simply. "We went to the University of Texas together."

Jessie intensified the displeased expression she aimed at Byron. Why had he brought up college? Now Jake would certainly wonder why she was working at Ray's Cantina.

Since Jessie didn't think Jake would leave the room anytime soon, she dropped down onto the sofa and tried not to scream. The conversation would be like dancing barefoot on broken glass. There was plenty that Byron knew that Jake didn't and vice versa.

"If I'm not mistaken," she said coolly to Byron. "I asked you not to come here."

His smile was one of pure defiance. "I had to make sure you were all right."

"Well, as you can see, I'm fine." It was a huge lie, but Jessie didn't want to get into a detailed explanation.

There were times, like now, when she wished Byron didn't feel so protective. It was a chilling reminder of the conclusions she'd drawn about Willa. Overly protective people often did stupid things. She could recall at least a half-dozen occasions when Byron had resorted to fistfights when men had come on to Christy. Of course, that likely had something to do with his own feelings for Christy. Love and jealousy were usually a volatile mix.

"You don't look fine at all, Jess," Byron readily disagreed. "You look like hell. You're too thin, too pale—and what the devil happened to your hair?"

She wasn't about to get into that. The less Byron heard about her ordeal, the better. He obviously didn't need anything else to rile him. "I don't think you came here to discuss my weight or my current hairstyle.''

"No, I didn't." Byron looked up at Jake. "I heard someone shot at you. And at Jess. I don't like that. I don't like that you put her in danger.''

Because Jake was behind her and couldn't see her face, Jessie rolled her eyes and glared at Byron. "It isn't Jake's responsibility to keep me safe," she clarified. "Nor is it yours. I can take care of myself.''

"Now that makes me feel a whole lot better. This from a woman who was kidnapped and held against her will for three months. You couldn't take care of yourself then, could you, Jess? And now you're pregnant." Byron swore ripely and shook his head. "Pregnant. Jesus! Have you considered what else those SOBs could have done to you while they had you captive?''

"I've given it some thought, yes, but as you can see, I'm very much alive." She paused and tried to speak calmly. "Listen, Byron, I can't have you involved in this. I don't know what these people want, but it isn't good—and I don't think they're finished yet.''

"And that's why I'm here. I can help you.''

"How?" Jake firmly asked. There was a challenge in his tone. *What could you possibly do that I can't?*

"I can help locate the people who kidnapped her.''

Jake walked from behind her and faced Byron head-on. "One's dead. I have someone looking for the others. When they find them, Jessie and I will get to the bottom of this. What I want to know is, did you leak information, either accidentally or otherwise, that nearly got us killed?''

"What?" An angry flush swept over Byron's face. "How dare you accuse me of trying to hurt Jessie."

"I'm not accusing you of anything. I just want answers."

"And you think I have them?" Byron shouted back. "That's why I'm here. I want her safe. And I damn sure won't trust you for that. Besides, even if I trusted you, I could still do a better job of getting to the bottom of this. I'm a cop, remember?"

"Well, that hasn't stopped Jessie from nearly getting killed. Why haven't you conducted an investigation, if you're so concerned about her?"

"This isn't my case. Or my jurisdiction. That doesn't mean I haven't looked into things. Care to know my theory? You're behind this, McClendon. And now you've managed to convince Jessie that you're the good guy, that you're on her side. Well, I don't believe it for a minute. I don't like it when people try to hurt my friends."

Jessie got to her feet. This situation wouldn't get better. The two men had squared off like barking dogs defending their territories. She quickly latched on to Byron's arm. "It's time you left. Come on, I'll see you out."

"I don't want—"

"Tough." She yanked harder and got him moving. Jessie didn't say anything else until they were at the door. She only hoped Jake was out of hearing range. "Do you want to make this more difficult for me?"

"That's a dirty way to win an argument."

"Maybe, but I'm not going to let you accuse Jake of God knows what."

That didn't please Byron and it was obvious. His mouth tightened. "You're falling for him, aren't you.'' But he didn't even wait for her to deny it. ''God, Jess! This is the kind of stunt Christy would have pulled, not you. You were always the sensible one.''

''It's not a stunt.'' She lowered her voice to a whisper. ''Jake's bent over backward to help me.''

Fortunately, Byron lowered his voice, as well. ''Oh, yeah? Think back to the last time you spoke to Christy. She all but said she was going to throw herself at McClendon. A few hours later, she was dead.''

''I believe that was a coincidence.''

Anger and frustration clouded his expression. In fact, it did more than cloud it. Jessie watched the veins throb on his forehead. ''Well, I'm tired of the two of you getting yourselves in these stupid fixes,'' he snapped.

Alarmed, she pulled back her shoulders. ''The two of you?'' she repeated. ''Do you mean Christy and me? What are you talking about, Byron?''

Something darkened his eyes. Confusion, maybe. And then he shook his head. ''I'm sorry. I shouldn't have said that.'' He reached in his jacket, brought out a fat envelope and handed it to her. ''Your money, all fifteen thousand.''

It was literally her life savings. But it wasn't the money that held her attention. It was Byron's remark. *I'm tired of the two of you getting yourselves in these stupid fixes.* What had he meant by that?

Nothing, she quickly assured herself. Absolutely nothing.

''Take my advice, Jess,'' Byron added. He stepped outside into the darkness and headed for his car.

"Use that money and get the hell away from Mc-Clendon before it's too late."

It was already too late for a lot of things, but Jessie wished there was some way Byron could take back that off-the-cuff comment. It would stay with her. And haunt her.

"Too bad you didn't tell me your friend was a cop," Jake said the moment she turned around. He was in the foyer, obviously waiting for her.

One glance and she knew he wasn't a happy man. With reason. Byron's visit had likely created a lot of questions. Questions she might not want to answer. However, instead of asking her anything, he reached into his pocket and pulled out a tiny phone.

"Make sure Detective DuCiel leaves the grounds," Jake told the person he called. "And secure the gate behind him." After what seemed to be an eternity, his gaze slowly came to her again. "Has he found out anything about your kidnapping that I should know?"

"No." She closed the door and folded her arms over her chest. "He checked out the warehouse but didn't come up with anything."

Jake tipped his head to the envelope she still held in her hand. "And the money I heard Byron mention—what's that all about?"

"It's from my savings account. I'll need it to relocate."

Jessie walked closer and thought about putting her hand on his arm. She changed her mind when she saw the anger flash in his eyes. Instead, she went back into the living room. As she'd known he would do, Jake followed her.

"Listen, this isn't anything new," she explained.

"I have to leave eventually. You're in the middle of a campaign and if the press gets wind that I'm staying with you, it could hurt your chances in the election."

"I'm not married. I'm allowed to have female houseguests without having to explain it to everyone."

"Still, I'm not comfortable with this." Jessie took a deep breath. "I've thought about asking the police to put me in protective custody."

"Whoever's behind this has connections," he pointed out. "Perhaps even to the police."

Yes, perhaps. And it was a brutal reminder of the conversation she'd just had with Byron. Jessie was almost afraid to let the next question form in her mind. But she couldn't stop it. No matter how hard she tried, she couldn't stop it.

Was it possible she'd been wrong about Byron?

God, was it possible?

Chapter Twelve

Frustrated that his questions about Byron would obviously have to wait, Jake yanked the phone from his pocket when it started to ring. "McClendon."

"Thank God," the woman said in a near whisper. "I didn't know who would answer this line."

"Who is this?" Jake demanded.

"I'm not sure you'll remember me."

Oh, yes he did. It'd been a while since Jake had heard that voice, but he knew exactly who she was. He just couldn't believe they'd finally, maybe, gotten a break. "Marion Cameron. You were a nurse at Cryogen Labs." And one of the people no doubt responsible for Jessie's kidnapping.

Jake motioned for Jessie to move closer. He grabbed the notepad off the table and wrote the caller's name. Jessie's eyes widened when she read it. She frantically motioned for him to continue the conversation.

"What can I do for you, Ms. Cameron?"

"I have some things to tell you, but first I need a promise that you'll give me protection. I won't say another word unless you can swear to me that you won't let them kill me."

Jessie put her ear close to his so she could hear. "I promise I'll do my best to protect you," Jake assured her. After all, he very much needed her alive so he could find out what she knew. "Where are you?"

Her voice crumbled and it took her several moments to steady it. "I'm just outside the security gate at your ranch."

God, she was right under his nose. Jake immediately thought of Detective DuCiel. He hoped DuCiel had already made it off the property so the woman wouldn't be spooked. He also hoped the ranch hand had secured the gate as Jake had told him to do. He didn't want Marion Cameron just driving up to the front door. And he also couldn't risk her bringing in those two guards who'd held Jessie hostage.

With the phone pressed to his ear, Jake started toward the door. Unfortunately, Jessie followed him.

"I'm coming to get you," he told Marion. *"Alone."*

"I've done some terrible things," Marion continued. "Stupid things. I'm sorry."

"Sorry for what? What do you mean?" Jake wanted to hear everything she had to say, but he wanted to hear it face-to-face.

He made it to the front door and grabbed a gun from the entry closet before he turned around and placed his hand on Jessie's shoulder. *You're staying here,* he mouthed.

She frantically shook her head.

The woman on the other end of the line made a strangled sound as if choking back tears. "There's a plot to ruin you."

Nothing new there. Jake had already come to that conclusion.

He turned to leave, but again Jessie followed him. She just brushed off his hand when he put it on her shoulder. Jake didn't have time to waste on this battle of wills. He needed to get to the gate before the woman left.

"Why do you want to ruin me?" he asked Marion. He hurried outside, taking the steps two at a time. Jessie stayed right behind him. He gave her a look that she wouldn't have any trouble interpreting—*stay back*. But she didn't stay back. When he got into the car, she climbed into the passenger seat, slid right next to him and put her ear close to the phone.

"It wasn't me who wanted to ruin you," Marion continued. "I didn't know what they'd planned to do. I swear, I didn't. Dr. Radelman said no one would get hurt. I needed the money, you see. My husband wiped out our accounts. I had bills to pay. I was going to lose my home."

Jake started the car and pulled away from the house. He easily could have taken the paths through the woods and run there, if Jessie hadn't been with him. But since she insisted on going, the car might give her some protection if Marion was armed.

"We took this woman," Marion went on. "Dr. Radelman and I inseminated her. But he swore to me that she wouldn't be harmed."

Jake gripped the steering wheel hard and tried to block out the image of Jessie locked up in that warehouse. Three months of hell they'd put her through. There was no way he could forgive Ms. Cameron for being part of that.

"Who chose this woman?" Jake asked. Because

Jessie was so close to him, he could feel the pulse drum in her body.

"Jessie. That's her name. Jessie Barrett. I don't know who chose her or why. Dr. Radelman had her address, her name. I don't know how he got it."

So it probably wasn't random. They'd chosen Jessie for a reason. He was sure if he learned that reason, he could figure out who was behind this. "Why did you want this woman inseminated?"

"Dr. Radelman said it would ruin you. We did some tests. The DNA will prove it's your child, and we were supposed to leak that information to the press."

Again, that was nothing new. He'd known this was his child. Still, it was a jolt to hear her say it. Beside him, Jessie pulled in her breath.

Jake stopped the car a good quarter of a mile from the gate. It was as close as he wanted Jessie to get to this woman.

"Who's behind this plan—Radelman?" he asked.

"No. He was just like me. He did it for the money, too."

"Then, who? Abel Markham?"

"I don't know. I truly don't know. There were two guards. They brought us our money. In cash. I only knew them by their first names—Mike and Lennie. They traded off shifts. Don't bother looking for them. If Dr. Radelman is dead, they probably are, too."

Jake would put money on it. "Why would your boss want them dead? For that matter, why would he want Radelman dead? If all he wanted to do was ruin my campaign—"

"God, no," the woman interrupted. "It wasn't to ruin your campaign. It was to ruin *you*."

He shook his head. "I don't understand."

She made a pitiful sound. A ragged sob. "After we leaked the DNA results to the press, the guards had orders to kill Jessie. I didn't know. I swear I didn't know. They were going to strangle her and leave her body where someone could find it."

Jake felt as if someone had knocked the breath right out of him. It was true. It was all true. He choked back everything he was feeling—the hate, the rage, the fear—and forced himself to keep talking. "Why did they want her dead?"

"So you'd be blamed for her murder. It would give you motive, you see. Because she worked at that bar and because the test would prove the baby was yours. They'd say you murdered her because she was carrying your child."

Jake balled up his fist and pressed it against his head. He fired a glance at Jessie. She was ashy pale and her bottom lip trembled. He caught her around the waist and pulled her to him. She whispered something. His name, he realized. And she wrapped her arm around him.

"I didn't know they were going to kill her until I heard them talking about it," Marion continued. "That's when I left the door unlocked so she could escape. But I think they found her. She was drugged. I'm sure they found her. I was trying to save her and the baby."

Jessie's grip tightened, but he eased her away from him. There wasn't time to comfort her now. Marion Cameron was the only witness they had, and he needed to get to her.

Jake grabbed his gun and motioned for Jessie to stay put when he opened the car door. He aimed a finger at her stomach to remind her that she needed to think of the baby. She finally seemed to listen, though she folded her arms over her chest and glared at him. What she didn't do was get out of the car when he did.

He held his hand over the phone so Marion couldn't hear what he whispered to Jessie. "If anything goes wrong, promise me that you'll get out of here." When she didn't say anything, he repeated it.

Jessie nodded eventually. He paused a moment until her eyes came to his. There was no time to wish he'd forced her to stay at the house. No time to wish he'd alerted one of the ranch hands to come and stay with her. He prayed those wouldn't be mistakes that he would soon regret.

"I can arrange protection for you," he told Ms. Cameron. He reached over, opened the glove compartment and pulled out a gun. Jake figured Jessie knew how to use one, since she'd owned a couple of .38s. He pressed the weapon into her hands. It was paltry protection against someone who seemed ready to go to all lengths to kill her, but it was all he could offer.

He held Jessie's gaze a moment longer and saw the swirl of so many emotions. Fear, concern, and even hope. Hope that the threats on her life would soon come to an end.

"Be careful," she murmured.

He nodded. "You, too."

Her mouth opened as if she was about to say something else, but she didn't. Jessie shook her head, a frustrated gesture that he understood all too well.

Jake forced himself to tear his gaze away and he hurried toward the gate. "You need to tell the police everything you just told me," he explained to Marion.

"I will, I promise. Just come and get me before someone else finds out that I'm here. I don't want to die, Mr. McClendon. If they—" And just like that, she hung up.

Hell. He hadn't wanted her to do that. He'd wanted to keep her on the line to make sure she didn't change her mind. Marion Cameron was the only living link he had to the person who'd kidnapped Jessie.

Jake ran the rest of the way. He saw the dark-colored car parked on the side of the road and the woman behind the wheel. Not Byron. Evidently, he was long gone. And so was the ranch hand who'd escorted him out.

Not wanting to leave the gate open, Jake decided to scale it, instead. It would set off the silent alarm that would alert the security company, but that wasn't such a bad idea. He climbed up the wrought-iron panel and dropped to the ground on the other side.

The moment his feet touched the ground, he heard Marion start the car. He also heard the odd noise that came from the thick woods to his right. God, someone was out there.

There was a *swish* that made his mouth turn to dust. Jake dived behind a cluster of bushes. He couldn't be sure, but he thought maybe someone had fired a shot from a rifle rigged with a silencer.

Marion must have seen or heard something, as well. She gunned the engine, kicking up dirt when she clipped the ditch. Somehow she managed to get the car back on the road and turned around. She sped away.

He scrambled to his feet, torn between going after Marion or running back to make sure Jessie was all right. It wasn't even really a decision. He only prayed that it wasn't too late.

WITH HER HAND CLAMPED around the gun, Jessie watched for any sign of Jake. Nothing. But then, he'd only been gone a few minutes. Mercy, the waiting was always the hardest part, especially with Marion's words still ringing in her head.

Jessie had known someone wanted her dead, but to hear it chilled her to the bone. Because they hadn't just wanted her dead. They wanted to set up Jake to take the blame. They would murder her to ruin him. In the grand scheme of things, the baby and she were nothing more than expendable casualties.

She stared out into the darkness. No sign of Jake. No sign of anyone. Not even the dogs were around. She almost wished they were. Even though they frightened her, they would alert her if something was wrong.

It hit Jessie then. She'd been so caught up in worrying about Jake and rehashing the plot to kill her that she hadn't considered the other things Marion had said. Jake had just learned the DNA would prove that this was his child.

His child.

Jessie caught her bottom lip between her teeth. He hadn't believed her when she told him about the baby. Did he believe Marion Cameron? Were her words eating away at him or had he found some way in his mind to deny it?

Yes, that was probably it.

Right now, Jake was most likely trying to rationalize all of this away. And why not? Ms. Cameron's confession wasn't necessarily gospel. She had simply repeated what she'd been told. What if Markham or the person behind this planned to fix the DNA evidence to reveal what he wanted it to reveal? Suppose Jake's vials really had been destroyed at Cryogen Labs?

Jessie ran her hand over her stomach. There was a baby inside her, a baby with no father. Even if it was Jake's DNA that had been forced to join with hers, it didn't make him the father. DNA couldn't do that. That had to come from the heart. And she wouldn't force this on him, even if she wanted it.

She didn't.

Jessie blinked hard when her eyes started to water. It was good that Jake would likely dismiss all of this. That way, she could leave and eventually get on with her life. The truth of the DNA didn't matter to her. This baby had no father, but it had a mother. And she would make sure that was enough.

It would just have to be enough.

She leaned closer to the window when she thought she heard something. An odd sound. Someone running, maybe. Or maybe just the breeze rustling through the leaves. Her gaze raked through the heavily wooded area that surrounded her.

Nothing.

Jessie released the breath she'd been holding and sank lower into the seat so that she wasn't so visible. She was inside the security gates, she reminded herself. Jake had said there were sensors all around the property. So if anyone tried to get in, they would trip the alarms. That didn't give her as much peace of mind as she would have hoped. After all, Byron had gotten through and so had Markham. Douglas and Willa obviously had access, as well.

Trying not to let her fears get the best of her, she forced herself to concentrate on Jake. By now, he had certainly reached Marion and was, Jessie hoped, already on his way back. While she was hoping, Jessie silently added a prayer that he would stay safe, that all of this would work out without anyone else getting hurt. At the moment, it seemed a lot to ask for.

There was another rustle, and just like that, her heart was in her throat. Something was terribly wrong. She could feel it in her bones. Jessie searched the woods again. Still nothing. Not a sign of Jake.

With the gun gripped in her right hand, she eased over the console and slipped into the driver's seat. *If anything goes wrong, promise me that you'll get out of here,* Jake had said. She'd barely had time to repeat the words to herself, when the shot ripped through the glass, shattering the window on the passenger side where she'd been sitting just seconds earlier. Jessie heard the scream tear from her throat before she could stop it.

Oh God. Panic and fear raced through her, nearly choking off her breath. The bullet came so close, Jessie could feel it. Smell it. There'd been only a slight accompanying sound, however. That probably meant someone was using a silencer.

She twisted the key in the ignition, but before she could even put the car in gear, someone fired again. This shot demolished the back window and the rearview mirror. It sent a spray of glass and metal through the air. Jessie ducked. And threw the car into reverse.

The tires shrieked when she gunned the engine. She had to put some distance between her and the gunman. If not, the next time he probably wouldn't miss. As it was, he'd only missed her head by inches.

"Please," she prayed. And that prayer encompassed a lot. She had to get out of the line of fire, but she didn't want to do that at Jake's expense. She hoped he was still with Marion Cameron and wasn't anywhere near the shooter.

Her heart hammered. Her breath was ragged. Inside, her stomach churned, the fear nearly turning her inside out. With the gun still clutched in her hand, she used the side mirror to see the road. With the rear window a cracked web, it was her only chance of staying on the road.

There was nothing muffled about the next shot. It blistered through the air, and left her ears ringing with the terrifying sound. She didn't stop, didn't even look around to assess the damage, but the shot told her more than she wanted to know. The gunman had two weapons. At least. Guns rigged with night scopes or some other gadget that allowed him to shoot in the dark.

Another shot and Jessie felt the car jerk violently to the right. Someone had shot out the tire. God, he just wasn't giving up.

She grappled with the steering wheel, using all her strength to keep the car from careering out of control. One thing was for sure; she couldn't stay on the road where the gunman obviously had a clear line of sight. When she spotted a narrow clearing in the wooded area, Jessie went for it. Her arms strained and knotted, but somehow she got the car headed in that direction. She shot into a group of towering oaks, praying they would give her the cover she needed to survive.

The bullets didn't stop. One right after another, the shots slammed through the car, spewing the chunks of safety glass everywhere. Jessie fought the black wave of panic that washed through her. She couldn't give in to it. It would only make her powerless to help herself.

Fighting the steering wheel, she shoved her foot onto the accelerator, lurching the car ahead. She didn't dare turn on the headlights, but she could barely see inches ahead of her. The trees and underbrush were thick, practically smothering the narrow path. Still, she didn't have a choice but to go forward. She had to get away from the gunman and that high-powered rifle that he was using to hunt her down.

Hunt her down. Jessie mumbled the words aloud several times. For some reason, she thought of that photograph in the library. The one of Willa with the hunting rifle propped on her shoulder. She didn't want to believe Jake's sister would do something like this, but Willa did have a motive. And the means. Did she have the capacity to kill, as well?

Jessie had to put that thought aside. Quickly aside. The large oak limb she had thought was farther to her left, wasn't. It smashed into her side window, bringing a deluge of safety glass right into her lap. Rough, finger-like branches snagged her clothes. She didn't stop. She continued to maneuver the car deeper into the woods.

The cedars were suddenly so thick, she lost sight

of the path. She clipped one of the trees with her right fender, the metallic sound screeching through the night. And the silence. It was that silence that made her ease off the accelerator and bring the car to a stop. Just in time. Directly ahead of her, no more than three feet away, was a massive oak that completely blocked her way. Thank God, she hadn't hit it.

Fighting a strong instinct to run and at the same time trying not to make any sudden moves, Jessie released the steering wheel so she could better aim the gun. Dreading what she might see, she glanced around. There was nothing but woods—but then, she couldn't see very far. The person with that gun could be behind any one of the hundreds of trees.

Then she heard the sound.

Her throat clenched. Her chest pounded as if it might shatter. The panic that she'd tried to control was so close to the surface, she could feel it ripple over her skin.

It was the sound of someone running. This time, Jessie was sure of it. Was it Jake? Had he somehow maneuvered his way through all those shots to get to her? She hated to consider one alternative—that he hadn't made it through. Or the other alternative—that it wasn't Jake at all, but the person who wanted her dead.

She turned slowly in the direction of the sound. It was just as she feared. Someone was out there. Close. So close that she saw a flash of movement before the person darted behind a tree.

Jessie couldn't stop the shudder that racked her body and left her trembling. If this had just been about her, she could have faced it better. Her training might have given her the confidence to go on the offensive. But it wasn't just her. And going on the offensive, stepping out of the car to fire, could get her baby killed. Or Jake. Either way, she couldn't risk it.

Gripping the gun with both hands, she sat there. Moments. Long, excruciating moments. Waiting. For what, exactly, she didn't know. The only sound was her heart pounding in her ears and her breath coming in shreds.

"Jessie!" the voice called out.

It was Jake. She twisted in the seat, frantically searching through the thicket to see him. She couldn't. "I'm here," she answered, praying the sound of her voice didn't allow the gunman to pinpoint their positions.

But she heard only Jake.

"Jessie, are you all right?"

"Yes." At least, she thought she was. Glass was everywhere, even in her lap, but she didn't think she was wounded.

"I'm coming closer," Jake said.

She hadn't thought she could be more frightened, but that sent a cold chill through her. She didn't want him to get hurt. "Be careful! There's a gunman somewhere out here."

That obviously didn't stop Jake. He came tearing through the darkness, straight toward the driver's side of the car where she sat. Jessie had never been happier, and more terrified, to see anyone.

She shoved open the door and caught his arm, pulling him inside with her.

"Are you sure you're all right?" he demanded, his voice hoarse and rough.

She nodded, somehow. "What about you?"

"I'm not hurt."

And with that, Jake latched on to her and hauled her against him. In the same motion, his mouth came to hers. Not gentle. Not sweet. The kiss was filled with all the emotion their dangerous situation had created.

"I thought I'd lost you," Jake whispered against her mouth. His grip around her tightened.

Jessie wanted to assure him that he hadn't lost her, but she couldn't gather enough breath to speak. She held on to him and let the safety, the rightness, of Jake's embrace seep through her.

"Something went wrong," he explained. He put the car into reverse and pushed her down onto the seat. "Marion drove away, when someone fired a shot."

"Who? Did you see the gunman?"

"No, but at least some of those shots came from inside the property."

Yes. She'd known that, but it hadn't sunk in as to exactly what that meant. The alarms hadn't gone off. The dogs hadn't responded.

Jake began to back out of the narrow path. "Someone must have tampered with the security system."

And that someone was likely a person they knew. The thought terrified her, but as bad as that was, it was worse for Jake. If it hadn't been Markham or one of his people, then it was Douglas or Willa. Jake's family.

"Stay down," he warned, when she started to get up. "We're not taking any more chances. One way or another, I'm putting an end to this.'' There was no anger in his voice. Just sheer determination.

Jessie desperately wanted to believe him. She needed to believe him. Because the alternative was unthinkable.

Chapter Thirteen

He had a plan. Jake wasn't sure it was a good one, but it was what he finally came up with after sitting up half the night. If he got lucky, really lucky, it just might work. Now all he had to do was convince Jessie to go along with it.

That would probably take nothing short of a miracle.

Adjusting the breakfast tray in his hand, he knocked on her door. "It's me. Can I come in?" Jake asked.

A pause. A long one. "Sure."

Jessie sat up in bed when he walked in. She still wore the clothes she'd had on the night before, meaning she'd probably fallen asleep in them. With reason. It was late by the time they finished giving the police their statements about the most recent shooting and she'd been exhausted.

Jake was thankful that she looked rested now. And rumpled, with her dark hair fluffed around her face. Her eyes were still ripe with sleep. There was something about it that greatly appealed to him. Of course, most things about Jessie appealed to him.

"Breakfast," he announced. "Scrambled eggs,

toast, decaf coffee and orange juice.'' Jake placed the tray on her lap and sat on the bed next to her.

She studied each item. ''Thanks, but I doubt I'll be able to eat much.''

''Just a few bites, then.'' He pointed to the bottle of prenatal vitamins that Dr. Lisette had prescribed. ''I sent someone into San Antonio this morning to get these for you. By the way, how are you feeling?''

''All right, I guess. No light-headedness—but then, I haven't tried to stand up yet.''

''No morning sickness?''

''Not so far.'' She took a sip of the coffee, made a face and quickly put it aside. ''But I don't want to push it. Funny, I used to love coffee, but I don't think I'll be drinking much of it anytime soon.''

Jake took the cup off the tray and set it on the nightstand. ''Anne had morning sickness.'' He hadn't intended to say that. In fact, he hadn't intended to bring up his late wife at all.

''Willa talked about her,'' Jessie said hesitantly. ''She said Anne and the baby died in childbirth.''

''They did. Toxemia.'' Not the best subject to discuss with a pregnant woman. ''It's rare, and Anne had other complications that made the toxemia fatal. For both her and the baby.''

''Willa seemed to think you blame yourself.''

Jake didn't care much for the fact that his sister had apparently been a chatterbox when it came to his personal life. He'd have to discuss that with Willa later. ''I did.'' And he still did. There was no use bringing that up, either. Besides, this wasn't what he wanted to talk about. His plan—

''Why would you blame yourself?'' Jessie asked. ''What happened was a tragic accident.''

"Still, if I hadn't wanted a child…" There was no reason to finish that. Here, he'd just accused Willa of talking too much and he was doing the same thing. Jessie didn't need to hear any of this.

She picked up her fork and poked at the scrambled eggs. "I used to do that, you know."

Jake tried to lighten the mood. "What, play with your food?"

The corner of her mouth hitched into a short-lived smile. "I used to blame myself for my father's behavior. He'd come home drunk and beat my mother senseless, yell at me, call me names that I didn't even understand. I thought it was my fault. If I had just cleaned my room better. Or if I smiled when he walked in, instead of trying to hide somewhere until the storm passed."

A slow ache worked its way through his heart. Jake wished he had ten minutes alone with the man who'd caused her so much pain. "There was nothing you could have done. You were a child."

"I was never a child. He took that away from me." She took a deep breath. "Anyway, I'm getting off track. What happened with my father wasn't my fault any more than Anne's death was yours. Those things gave us scars. And they made us stronger. They made us the people we are today. Heck, if it weren't for my father, I'd probably never have become a—"

Jake stared at her when she stopped abruptly. She looked like a deer caught in headlights. "A what?" he asked.

"Uh, a better person. Besides, I've got a one-hundred-percent chance of being a better parent than my father was."

Jake waited another moment to see if she intended to feed him more bull. She apparently didn't. Jessie had nearly let something slip, but what? As much as he wanted to know, he knew he had bigger fish to fry.

"You're not eating," he pointed out.

"I'm not hungry."

"But you'll eat. For the baby."

"Yes, I suppose I will." She took a small bite of the scrambled eggs and made a sound to indicate they were good.

"What else would you be willing to do to make sure the baby is safe?" he asked.

Obviously surprised, she stared at him a moment. "Is this a hypothetical question or do you have something specific in mind?"

He shrugged. "Both."

"Well." She drank some of her orange juice. "I guess I'd do whatever's necessary."

"But you have to keep yourself safe in order to do that."

She nodded eventually, but her eyes narrowed in suspicion. "If you've got something to say, Jake, spit it out. It's not like you to beat around the bush."

True. It seemed odd that she would know that about him. Jessie had known him for less than a week and yet she had him pegged. Unfortunately, he had her pegged, too. She wouldn't like what he had to say.

"I have a proposal I'd like to make."

She picked up a piece of toast and idly peeled off the crust before she took a bite. "What kind of proposal?"

"*A* proposal." He studied her face and watched her expression turn from suspicion to confusion.

Jessie shook her head. "Sweet heaven, this must be something incredibly bad if you're acting like this. What do I have to do—run naked down Commerce Street or something?"

"Not quite." Even though he wouldn't mind seeing her run naked down the hallway to his bedroom. He took the toast from her hand and had a bite, too. "It's a proposal and you'd have to do what women generally do after they've received one." He paused, wondering if he should move that knife and fork a little farther away.

"And that would be what?"

"Accept."

"Accept," she repeated, obviously puzzled. The second time she repeated it, she didn't seem so puzzled. Her eyebrows drew together. The third time the word left her mouth, she shoved the tray off her lap and got to her feet. "Are you..." But she shook her head again. "No, you aren't."

"I am," he quickly assured. "I'm asking you to marry me." Jake held up his hand to stop her from interrupting him. "Well, actually, I have to insist that you agree to marry me."

Her mouth opened, but for several moments nothing came out. "Is this a joke?"

"It's the easiest way for us to keep you safe."

"Safe? What does that have to do with keeping me safe?" But she didn't wait for an answer. Jessie glanced at the bathroom door. "Could you excuse me a minute?" She bolted into the bathroom, slamming the door behind her. A moment later, Jake heard her retching.

Well, it wasn't exactly the response he'd hoped for. It certainly wasn't a thank you, even though he hadn't thought she would do that, either. Still, it did sting his pride a little. He'd offered her marriage. And she'd thrown up. He obviously had some kinks to work out of his plan.

Jake patted his pocket to make sure the ring he'd taken from his safe was there. It was. A ring that had belonged to his mother. Hopefully, Willa wouldn't pitch a fit when she saw it on Jessie's finger. And hopefully Jessie would actually let him put it on her finger.

Somehow, some way, he would make it work. Jake was afraid it was the only way he could keep Jessie and his child alive.

JESSIE LEANED OVER THE SINK and splashed some water on her face, intentionally dodging her reflection in the mirror. No use making matters worse. She no doubt looked exactly the way she felt. Sick. Stunned. And bewildered.

"Are you all right?" Jake called out from the other side of the door.

"Fine," she answered. But she wasn't. And the sudden bout of morning sickness was just a small part of it. This ridiculous notion that Jake had about marrying her was the main reason she'd lost her breakfast. Once she pulled herself together she would set him straight.

She sat on the edge of the bathtub and leaned her head against the smooth, cool tiles. It helped some but not nearly enough. Her head was light. Her skin still clammy. Maybe the crazy symptoms had caused her to misunderstand what Jake had said. Maybe he'd meant something other than marriage.

Or maybe not.

"Would you like me to come in there?" he asked. "I might be able to help. I could hold your head or something."

Jessie preferred clarification to head holding. Unfortunately, she wouldn't get it in the bathroom. That had to come from Jake. She dried her face and cautiously opened the door. He was right there leaning against the jamb, and there was obvious concern in his expression.

"I'm fine, really," she assured him.

He looked her over, paying careful attention to her eyes. "Would you like to lie down for a while?"

"We have to talk. I think we left off at the part where I was telling you that you've lost your mind." Jessie stepped around him and went back into the bedroom. She didn't want to get near the food, so she sat in the wicker chair near the balcony doors.

"I haven't lost anything. This makes sense. Besides, I didn't mean married exactly. More like engaged."

"Engaged," she repeated. Well, that was slightly better, but not much. Engaged was only a step away from the altar. "It wouldn't work."

"It's the perfect solution. The person who had you kidnapped wants to kill you and set me up for a murder charge."

"I know, Jake. I heard what Marion Cameron said, too." And just hearing it again made her stomach churn even more.

"Well, the only way that could work is for the police to believe I had a motive to kill you. They would have to believe I wanted to silence you because I got you pregnant."

Not just because he got *her* pregnant. But because he got a cocktail waitress pregnant.

"But if we're engaged," Jake continued, "then I have no motive. And if I don't have a motive, there's no reason for them to kill you."

Jessie looked for flaws in his logic. There had to be some part of it that didn't make sense. Wasn't there? Of course. But it took a while before she came up with it. "You have no proof that Ms. Cameron told us the truth."

"Why would she lie? What would she have to gain by calling me to let me know she'd had a part in your kidnapping?"

"I don't know, but I don't want to put my trust in a criminal."

"We don't have to trust her. If we're engaged it eliminates their inducement to kill you." He walked closer and stood directly in front of her. "You and the baby will be safe."

Would they? Jessie didn't want to jump on this without thinking it through. Would an engagement actually prevent the killer from coming after her? Perhaps. Maybe more than perhaps. And it wasn't as if the engagement would be real. Certainly, Jake wasn't proposing that.

She cleared her throat. "So what you're really suggesting is a pretend engagement?"

"It would only be pretend to us. Everyone else would have to believe it was true."

"Everyone, including the press and the voters?"

"Especially the press."

So here was the flaw Jessie had been looking for.

"But what about your campaign? This would destroy your chances of winning the election. Maybe that's why Marion called you. She must have figured you'd come to this conclusion and this is her way of still ruining you. Markham would still win."

It didn't make much sense when Jessie heard her own words. There was no way Marion could have known Jake would come up with a pretend engagement.

Jake shoved his hands in his pockets. "It wouldn't ruin the campaign, but we would have to go public right away. No mention of kidnapping or insemination, either. We'll just announce that we're engaged."

Apparently there would be no mention of falling in love, either. With reason, of course. He hadn't fallen in love. "You'll still lose votes."

"Some, but we won't have to worry about someone trying to kill us."

If he'd said *you* instead of *us*, Jessie would have had an argument. But he'd attached his safety to her decision.

"There has to be another way," she said under her breath.

"Believe me, I've thought about this, and we can't waste any more time. Someone drugged the dogs last night. And tampered with the security system. They walked right onto the property and took at least a dozen shots at us."

More reminders that she didn't need. And ones that sent her heart right back into her throat.

"There's a photographer on the way over here," Jake continued. "We can do the standard happy couple pose and he can have the pictures on the way to newspapers this afternoon.''

''That fast,'' she mumbled, getting to her feet.

''That fast. Later, I have a Citizens' Action Board dinner at the Sullivan Hotel, where we'll be spending the night. We can make the official announcement there, and tomorrow morning we can announce it again at the brunch with a local watchdog group. It's in the same hotel so it'll be easier for me to set up security.''

Jessie went through the plan and saw one obvious glaring contingency. Or rather two. ''This is just a guess, but this wasn't Douglas's or Willa's idea.''

She could tell from his bunched-up forehead what the answer was. ''They aren't pleased, but once I tell Willa the whole story, she'll come around. As for Douglas, eventually he'll look past how this affects the campaign. If not, it doesn't matter. I don't have the time to soothe their ruffled feathers right now. Later. When we've put the killer behind bars.''

So his family had given him plenty of grief. It wouldn't stop there either. His friends and constituents would feel the same way.

Jessie couldn't let him go any farther with this. It was past time for the truth. Once she'd told him she had been conducting an unauthorized investigation into Christy's death, Jake would quickly put aside this idea of a pretend engagement. Of course, he'd hate her, too, for not telling him the truth sooner. But maybe, just maybe, he wouldn't cause so much trouble that it would cost Byron his badge.

''There's more,'' Jake continued, before she could say anything. ''Marion Cameron is dead. The cops found her body in a motel off Interstate 35.''

The breath rushed out of her. She groped behind her for the chair arm and, when she located it, dropped onto the seat before her legs could give way. "She was murdered."

"She left a suicide note."

But Jessie wouldn't place a bet on the woman taking her own life. Like Dr. Radelman, she'd been killed. Either way, it didn't really matter. Suicide or murder, Marion was dead. That meant Jessie's link to finding her kidnapper was dead, too.

"Do you see now why it's so important that we make everyone believe we're engaged?" Jake asked. His voice was strained, as if each word struggled to get past his throat. "Don't think about what *you* want. Think about the baby. This person won't be merciful. He's killed at least two people and wouldn't hesitate to add you to the list."

It felt like another punch. Because it was true. She'd be killed and so would the baby. Jake would be framed for their murders. And she could stop it. She could stop it by simply saying yes.

"Make the arrangements," Jessie said softly. "We'll announce our engagement as soon as possible."

Without looking at her, Jake took her hand and slipped a ring on her finger. "You'll need this—"

It was a single square-cut diamond set in white gold. It caught the light and sent sparkles dancing over the room. It was also incredibly beautiful. She prayed it hadn't belonged to Anne, but she instinctively knew that it hadn't. Jake wouldn't have allowed her to wear Anne's engagement ring. That engagement was real. A promise to marry the woman he loved.

This engagement was strictly an arrangement. An arrangement that might save both of them and their child.

"Between now and tonight, you won't leave my side," he insisted. "And we won't trust anyone but each other. Understand?"

"Does that include Douglas and Willa?"

She saw the battle go on inside his head and saw the equally determined look in his eyes. "We only trust each other," he restated.

It was what she'd wanted to hear. Everyone was suspect.

"That includes your friend, Byron," Jake added.

"But—"

He pressed his fingertips over her mouth. "Everyone."

It wasn't even something she wanted to consider—that Byron had played some part in this. However, Jake must have felt the same way about Willa and Douglas.

"Everyone," she agreed.

But she prayed this pact wasn't necessary, that the killer was really Abel Markham. That was certainly better than the alternative. That the person who wanted them dead was someone they loved.

Chapter Fourteen

Jake cursed the cuff link that gave him so much trouble. He didn't need this tonight. He already had too much on his plate to be bothered by such trivial things.

He rapped once on the bedroom door before he pushed it open with his elbow. "Jessie, I have to go downstairs. I have to make sure—"

Jake looked up, the rest of what he should have said frozen somewhere between his throat and his mouth. She was there in the center of the room. Looking a little lost. Looking somewhat nervous. And absolutely stunning.

"Wow," he managed to say. Barely. The sight of her knocked most of the breath out of him.

Her nervousness showing, she touched her hair. "The stylist from the hotel salon came up and trimmed it for me. Willa bought the dress. You don't think the dress is too short?"

Oh, it was short, all right. Strapless. Midnight blue. And it fit her like skin. Jake was certain he wouldn't be the only man at the party who'd notice that. The well-above-the-knee dress was one unbroken surface of shimmering light, like tiny faceted sapphires glued to her body. He had a sudden urge to pluck them off one by one.

With his teeth.

"You look, uh, nice." Jake had to force out the understated compliment. He loosened his collar, hoping that would help. It didn't. Nothing short of eating his way through that dress would help.

"I don't know…" She looked in the mirror and smoothed her hands over the front of the dress. "It's not really me, you know?"

Yes, it was. It looked as if it had been designed with Jessie's slim body in mind. The only thing that appealed to him more was getting her out of the darn thing. "You'll dazzle everyone."

Her head snapped up, her gaze immediately fastening to his. Her eyes were wide and as brilliant as the dress. She obviously hadn't expected a compliment from him. Too bad the one he'd given her was pithy at best. Yes, she would dazzle everyone, but none as much as she'd already dazzled him.

She had her dark hair combed back from her face, but it didn't look stiff or overly styled. It was incredibly sexy. So was the thick band of liquid silver that she wore around her throat.

"Having trouble with that?" she asked.

For a moment he thought she'd looked at the front of his slacks. He was definitely having trouble in that area. But her attention was higher, on his cuff.

She walked to him, her stride confident despite the fact she wore thin high heels. Not quite stilettos, but they were high enough to give him a few fantasies. Of course, he hadn't needed the shoes to help him out with thoughts like those. He'd fantasized about her for days.

"Here, I can help." She eased the silver cuff from his fingers and began to push it through the hole. She shifted her body forward, and her hip brushed his thigh. "I'll try not to do anything that will draw attention to myself. Or anything that will embarrass you."

She was serious and apprehensive, but he couldn't give her the reassurance she obviously needed. Her simple touch had taken him from being semi-aroused to full-speed ahead.

Great.

Anybody with even partial eyesight would notice *that*. Talk about drawing attention to *himself*.

Jessie finished the cuff link and released his arm. Fidgeting, she adjusted his tie. "Should I hold your hand or anything when we're out there?" she asked.

Jake knew her question was innocent, but right now his thoughts weren't. They were somewhere in the nether regions of raunchy. "Just follow my lead. I want people to think we're engaged for all the usual reasons."

All in all, that would be easy to do. Right now, he felt very much like a sex-starved fiancé. Too bad the timing was stupid. He needed to be on his toes, and he damn sure had to think with his head and not another part of his body.

"I need to go into the ballroom first," he explained. "I want to make the announcement that we're engaged. Wait here until the guard escorts you down. Then I'll introduce you to some people."

She nodded. "I won't have to answer a lot of questions, will I?"

"No. Just smile and look..." His gaze traveled down her body. "All you have to do is smile." Hell, nobody would even hear the announcement once they got a good look at her. "After the introductions, we'll get out of there as fast as possible. I'd rather not have a crowd around you until we're sure the killer has gotten the message that you're not his next victim."

"That makes sense. Jake?" she said, when he started to leave. "Be careful, okay?"

"You, too." And he turned and left before he did something really stupid, like kiss her again. Because the next time he kissed her, he wasn't sure he could stop.

Hell, he wasn't sure he'd *want* to stop.

"ALL RIGHT, LET'S GET this show on the road," Willa said, when Jessie opened the door to the suite. But she wasn't alone. She lifted her hand to the man in the tux standing behind her. "This is your bodyguard. He's to escort us to the ballroom. Jake's orders."

Yes, Jessie had expected that. Jake had also mentioned there would be other undercover guards dispersed throughout the ballroom and the hotel.

Willa looked stunning in her slinky black gown, even with the formidable scowl on her face. It was a scowl that Jessie didn't think would go away anytime soon. Willa was obviously very unhappy about her brother's engagement. But then, Willa didn't know the whole story. She didn't know the engagement was fake. Well, she probably didn't. Jessie wasn't sure how much Douglas had told her.

Jessie gave her own dress one last look in the mirror. Blue silk and sequins. It was a far cry from her usual jeans. But then, so was the gelled hairstyle. She definitely didn't look like a pregnant woman in fear of her life.

"You're not in Kansas anymore, Dorothy," she mumbled as the three left the suite. She was somewhere between Buckingham Palace and the Twilight Zone. It wasn't likely to get better, either, with the party and announcement of her engagement to Jake.

Jessie tried to recall how long it'd been since she had attended a party, but she couldn't remember. There had been a get-together at the precinct for those working Christmas Day. It was nothing like what she thought she would face in that ballroom.

For one thing, she'd face Jake. In a tux.

Now that was a sure-fire way to get her pulse racing. How could any man possibly look that good in a glorified suit?

They stopped just outside the doorway of the ballroom, and Jessie peered inside. She didn't spot Jake because there was a sea of people in front of her. Jeweled gowns sparkled under the heavy chandeliers. The room smelled of champagne and expensive perfume.

"You'll have to excuse me a moment," Willa told her. "I need to find Douglas and let him know you're here."

"Sure."

Willa turned her attention to the guard. "And according to Jake, you're supposed to mingle while keeping an eye on Jessie."

With that tersely given cue, the man quietly stepped into the crowd. Conversation murmured throughout the room, stirring with the sound of a softly played piano. Nothing was overstated, except the underlying feel of old money.

Willa stared at her a moment longer. "Don't do anything to make this worse, all right?" Willa didn't even wait for Jessie to answer before she strolled away.

"You bet," she mumbled under her breath. Jessie was glad to have time to herself. Solitude wasn't something she'd had much of in the past few days, and despite the full-scale party going on, she'd never felt more alone in her life. Alone.

And vulnerable.

Jake's plan had to work. If not then she might as well tape a bull's-eye to her forehead. She was in the room with hundreds of people and any one of them could easily be the assassin hired to kill her. But that was only if Jake was wrong.

"I understand congratulations are in order, Ms. Barrett."

The speaker made her name sound like rattler venom and she turned around to face him. It was Abel Markham. He was dressed to kill in his tux and he had the look of a killer in his eyes. Jessie matched his glare. Markham was perhaps the pond scum responsible for the attempts on her life. And Jake's.

"I know who you are," Markham said simply. He sipped pungent-smelling whiskey, eyeing her over the rim of his glass. He eyed the dress, too. Funny, she hadn't felt self-conscious under Jake's intense scrutiny, but she sure did now.

"Oh?" Her glare probably took a nosedive with his remark, but she was anxious to hear what he had to say.

"You worked at Ray's Cantina and asked a lot of questions about the death of one of his employees. Christy Mendoza."

"So?" She glanced around, searching for Jake. He was nowhere in sight. However, she did spot the guard only about ten feet away. He lifted an eyebrow as if to ask if she needed help. She shook her head. Not that she particularly wanted to have this discussion with Markham, but it could prove enlightening.

"So I think it's strange that you'd become engaged to the man who was likely responsible for her death," Markham stated.

"The cops said it was an accident."

He smiled. It was slow and evil, and made goose bumps rise on her skin. "Then why were you asking the questions if you believed that?"

It was time to stop this game of cat and mouse. "How did you know I asked about this woman, anyway?"

His expression never faltered. "Ray is an acquaintance."

"Oh, yeah?" Jessie ran her cop's gaze over his face. And she took her time. "You don't look like the sort of man who'd admit to knowing Ray. It's hard to believe you and I have something in common."

His smile eased away. "Be careful, Ms. Barrett."

"Of what?" she asked boldly.

"Of whom you trust. If your soon-to-be husband didn't kill that woman, he's no doubt covering for someone who did. If I were you, I'd look at Douglas Harland or even Willa. Douglas's womanizing is common knowledge. Maybe Willa finally got fed up and eliminated her competition."

Jessie wouldn't dare let him know that he'd made a direct hit with that accusation. It was the main reason she'd begun her undercover investigation. All along, she'd felt that someone had covered up Christy's death.

"Where's Willa?" Jake asked.

Jessie whirled around to face him. He was not a happy man, and all that unhappiness was aimed at Abel Markham. "She went to find Douglas," Jessie told him.

Jake kept his stony gaze on the other man when he spoke. "She shouldn't have left you alone. No telling what might come crawling in here." He put a firm grip on her arm and led her away from Markham. "I don't want you talking to him, understand?"

"Believe me, it wasn't planned."

"Did he say anything to upset you?"

"No." She wouldn't mention that he'd all but implicated Jake, Douglas and Willa in a possible murder and cover-up. Besides, the room was packed— not the ideal place to discuss anything that might be overheard by the wrong person.

Jake forced a smile as a couple approached them. "We'll talk about that later. Mr. and Mrs. Emmett, I'd like for you to meet my fiancée, Jessie Barrett."

Jessie greeted them, but out of the corner of her eye she watched the transformation in Jake. He slid right into the role of the soon-to-be groom, merging it with that charismatic politician persona. He smiled at the right moment. The nod was perfectly timed, as well. And so was the gentle caress he gave her bare shoulder. Style, class and just a touch of Texas arrogance.

He would break her heart, of course. He'd have no choice. This was his world. Silk, champagne and grand parties. She didn't belong here. She was a temporary glitch in his otherwise occasionally glitched life.

Jake led her to another group of people, the introductions passing in and out of her short-term memory. All eyed her curiously, but none said anything other than the niceties suitable for greeting a newly engaged couple.

"Would you like to dance?" Jake whispered.

He might as well have asked her if she wanted to bungee jump. She hadn't danced in years, and never in a ballroom. Jessie was about to decline when he added, "I want to hear what Markham had to say."

Of course. Somehow she'd almost forgotten. And dancing was probably the only way they would be able to have a private conversation.

Jake took her hand slowly, as if he had all the time in the world. He coupled their fingers and circled his arm around her waist, edging her to him. The music was soft and unhurried. He followed it and led her into the lazy rhythm of the dance. They moved together, like one. Body against body. Man and woman.

"Well?" he asked softly.

Jessie forced herself out of the romantic trance. The dance was fake, like their engagement. What Jake really wanted from her was information about Markham. "We didn't talk that long," she started.

She took a deep breath. Jake's scent was all around her. On her. Jessie moved her mouth closer to his ear. So he could hear her better, she rationalized. It occurred to her that a sudden turn in the dance step just might allow her lips to brush his skin. She wanted that. As ridiculous as it was, she wanted that cheap thrill.

"Markham admitted he knows Ray, the owner of the cantina where I worked," Jessie continued. "That could explain how he picked me for his victim. I'm sure Ray would have handed over my address and anything else Markham wanted to know. I'll bet if you look deep into their financial records, they've crossed paths before all of this—"

It happened. Someone on the dance floor bumped into them. Just an accidental nudge. Jessie's mouth glanced off his jaw. She didn't have time to savor her small pleasure; she felt the difference in Jake's posture immediately. His hand on her back tensed. She heard the whisper-soft groan rumble in his chest. Her body responded, too, to those subtle changes in his. A heat spread through her.

"Is that all Markham said?" Jake asked.

Was it? No. She had trouble concentrating again. "He tried to make me believe that you, Willa or Douglas was probably responsible for Christy Mendoza's death."

"Did he succeed?"

Jessie pulled back slightly so she could look at him. Now she didn't just have the distraction of his scent; there was that mouth. And those intense blue eyes. "Succeed at what?"

"In convincing you that one of us killed Ms. Mendoza."

She shook her head. "No. The only thing he convinced me of was that he's a dangerous man." And because Jessie thought they needed some levity, she added, "I hope you kick his butt in the election."

They shared a smile. Brief. Strained. But a smile nonetheless. "Are you ready to go back to the suite?'' Jake asked. "I think we've made our point. Markham knows he can't get to you now."

Yes, and that *was* the point. Jessie forced herself to repeat it to herself. The dance, the engagement, everything that had happened tonight was about making the killer understand that he couldn't afford to continue his plan. Only time would tell if they succeeded.

Jake started the farewells, letting everyone know they were about to turn in for the night. That's when it occurred to Jessie. He was taking her to their suite, which was a fancy word for a bedroom. A place with a bed.

She mentally shrugged. It didn't matter. Really. Sure, they'd kissed before. French kissed. And touched. They'd also come pretty darn close to stripping off their clothes when they were in the bedroom at the ranch. But tonight wasn't about things like that. Tonight Jake was waiting to see what would happen with the plot to kill her.

The last thing on his mind would be making love. With her.

And the last thing that should be on her mind was making love with him.

Chapter Fifteen

Jake glanced at the bottle of champagne chilling in the bucket. A gift from the hotel probably. To congratulate them on their engagement. Well, he doubted either of them would drink it. Jessie probably wouldn't indulge because of the baby. He wouldn't because he needed every shred of self-control to keep his hands off her.

Of course, it wasn't just his hands that itched to touch her. There were other parts of him especially obsessed with the idea.

His clothes were suddenly too tight and damn uncomfortable. He yanked off his jacket and tie, dropping them over the back of the sofa. Jake tackled the cuff links next. Then his shoes. He had his shirt halfway unbuttoned and was in the bedroom before he realized Jessie was watching him.

She stood in the doorway that separated the bedroom from the rest of the suite, as if there were some kind of invisible barrier stopping her. Her head was tilted to the side, the toe of one shoe tucked behind the slim heel of the other. She was playing with the loose strands of hair that fell on her neck. The pose was provocative—but then, he had a one-track mind tonight.

"Do you want to take the sofa or should I?" she asked. He heard her swallow. Heard the soft intake of breath that followed.

"I'll take the sofa." But Jake immediately shook his head. "Look, this isn't going to work."

"All right. Then, I'll take the sofa. It really doesn't matter to me. I can sleep just about anywhere."

He intended to correct her, intended to tell her that he hadn't meant their sleeping arrangement. The real problem was, he couldn't be alone with her like this. He didn't trust himself. His answer, however, never made it out of his mouth. That's because he looked at her, and his resolve, his answer, flew out the eighth-floor window.

The room behind her was creamy white, even the carpet. The door frame was the same neutral shade. She was the only spot of color. Her dress seemed a sleek column of blue flames. And it paled in comparison to the woman who wore it. She looked like the answer to every prayer he'd ever said, to every hot fantasy he'd ever had.

Their eyes met. Hers were wide, a swirl of emotions in them. Jake sorted through those emotions. The uneasiness. The uncertainty. And finally saw what he'd known all along would be there. Desire. Passion. Need. It matched his own and shimmered like fire in Jessie's eyes.

He said her name, a ragged plea for her to be there for him when he made it to the other side of the room. Her answer was a thin, feminine response—a sigh mixed with a little flutter of breath. It was the most erotic sound he had ever heard.

Jake took a step toward her. Then another. At some point, even before he reached her, he quit trying to talk himself out of what he was about to do. No amount of talking would convince him to stop. This, whatever it was between them, had gone too far for either of them to turn back now.

She reached for him, catching his forearm at the same moment that he reached for her. They both closed the already narrow distance between them. Their bodies met. His crisp shirt and slacks whispered over the delicate blue fabric. And they came together in a lovers' embrace.

He skimmed his hand over the back of her dress. An interesting sensation. Cool silk, smooth sequins. Beneath that, he felt her stir. That was the most interesting sensation of all. Jessie, warm and trembling. Her, responding to his touch.

Taking his time, Jake eased his mouth to hers. A brush. A caress. A kiss. Her lips were damp and yielding. Receptive. She moaned softly against his mouth and let him touch the tip of her tongue.

"Should I take off my dress?" she whispered.

She obviously didn't have a clue what he had in mind. This wouldn't be some quick flash of fire that was over in a couple of minutes. He wanted a slow burn. Smoldering heat. He wanted to touch and taste. And he wanted to take the time to savor every inch of her.

"I'll undress you," he murmured. "Later."

"Well, that won't take much effort. The bra didn't fit, so it's still in the box in the bathroom. The stockings only go to mid-thigh, and there isn't even a garter belt. I don't know how the darn things stayed up when we danced. And to top it all off, my panties

are just a little swatch of thin blue lace. They'll probably disintegrate the minute you touch them."

"Damn." He ground out the word. The choke
hold he had on his desire crashed and burned. Jake
clenched his teeth together. He kissed her again, not
as gently as he'd planned. This time he touched more
than the tip of her tongue. The kiss was hard, hungry.
And deep.

Jessie responded. She made a sound of sheer pleasure and slipped her hand to the back of his neck.

He snapped her to him, catching on to her hips so
he could align them. Even through their clothes, he
could feel her puckered nipples. He felt her soft feminine body. She obviously felt him, as well, because
she rubbed against his arousal.

That did it. There was nothing left of that choke
hold.

"There's been a change of plans." Jake backed
toward the bed, never breaking the lock he had on
her. "I'll make love to you later. That dress comes
off now."

He sank onto the foot of the overly soft mattress,
reaching for her zipper in the same motion. Jessie
stepped between his legs and went after his clothes.
She was as tenacious as he was. She jerked the sides
of his shirt open and shoved it off him.

His hands were impatient, close to groping, but he
managed to get her zipper to slide down. Then the
dress. It slipped like blue oil off her body. Jessie
stepped out of it, but then she immediately placed
her arm over her breasts, covering herself.

"No." Jake shook his head. "Don't." And since
that seemed to be the extent of his vocabulary, he

took her arm and eased it away. Boy. What the heck
had he done to deserve this?

His gaze traveled down her body. Her breasts were
beautiful, small, and tipped with dark rose-colored
nipples. Her stomach, flat. She'd been right about the
panties. Thin. Blue. Flimsy. And the stockings. Oh,
the stockings. There was about a six-inch gap between the tops of them and her panties. That was six
inches times two of creamy female skin showing.
Bare skin.

He only glanced at the heels. Arousing, definitely.
And the panties that had already caused a frenzy. He
could see exactly what he wanted through the lace.

Jake cursed softly and shook her head.

"I told you," she whispered. "They'll fall apart
at the first touch."

Yes, the panties would. And he just might do the
same.

He looked up at her, snared her smoky gray eyes
and laid his hand on her stomach. She was the
mother of his child. That touched a different part of
him, but it had nothing to do with what he felt for
her now. This wasn't about the baby. This was about
Jessie. About them.

He lowered his hand and with one finger he traced
the outline of the lace, until he watched her eyelids
flutter. He did it again, this time pausing at the nar-
rowest point of the *V*. Her breath hitched. Her bottom
lip trembled. She pleaded for more.

He gave her more. Jake pressed his mouth to her
stomach, circling her navel with his tongue.

"Yes." Jessie fisted her hands in his hair. "Yes."

He went slightly lower. Kissed. Tasted. Lingered.
Keeping his gaze on her, Jake located the triangle of

lace again. When his mouth touched her through that fragile barrier, her back bowed and her eyes glazed. Jessie automatically slid her knee forward against his chest, anchoring it over his arm. She pushed her body closer. And closer.

"Please," she murmured.

She leaned to the side, obviously trying to get to the bed. Jake didn't let her. He had something different in mind.

One pull and the panties tore. Like the dress, they slipped right off, eliminating the only obstacle that stood in his way. He had to shake his head, fighting off the scent of arousal pulsing from her. He didn't want to be rough. Didn't want her to know he had almost no control left.

He touched her again with his mouth. With nothing between them. Nothing to prevent him from tasting her. This time he used his tongue and lingered, pleasing himself. Obviously pleasing her.

"Jake." She said his name frantically, as if calling for help. "Jake, please."

He didn't stop, even when her fingers dug into his shoulders. Jessie didn't pull away from him, either. She stayed, pressed close, whispering a mixture of honeyed words and profanity. In one breath, she worshipped him. Even loved him. In the next she threatened him if he stopped.

And with one cleverly placed brush of his tongue, he sent her straight over the edge.

She half moaned, half gasped, and leaned forward. Jake caught her in his arms and eased her onto the bed so he could see her face. Oh yes, she'd gone to the stars, all right. She had the misty, unfocused look of a woman who didn't know what the heck had just hit her. If he hadn't ached to be inside her, he might have savored that look for a while. But he was beyond that. Beyond just wanting her.

He freed himself from his slacks, not even taking the time to remove them. "Are you ready for me, Jessie?"

She lifted her head a fraction. "Yes, yes." Jessie reached for him, pulling him down on top of her.

Jake took off her shoes and tossed them on the floor. Legs and arms moved, adjusted, until he was exactly where he wanted to be. Wrapped in Jessie's arms.

He entered her slowly, easing into that tight feminine heat while her body still pulsed. Sweat glistened on her skin. Her breath was warm and moist on his neck. Jake whispered her name so she would look at him. She did. Her eyes were as hot and welcoming as the place where they joined so intimately.

She lifted her hips. Took him deeper. Embraced him. Held him in that silken grip of sensations so primal, so necessary. So familiar. And yet like nothing he'd ever felt. It roared through him. The need fused with the want. The want fused with something he'd thought he might never feel again. He couldn't even manage the profanity or the honeyed words that Jessie had.

He buried his face in her hair and let her take him to the only place he wanted to go.

JESSIE LET HERSELF float back to earth, but she didn't rush it. There'd be plenty of time for reality later. For just a little longer, she wanted to savor this feeling.

Jake was still on top of her. They were joined in

nearly every way possible. Somehow he'd managed to keep his pants on through all of it. She, on the other hand, was naked except for her stockings.

"I'll get off you in a minute," he mumbled. "When I can move."

"No hurry."

But apparently there was a hurry for him. Jake rolled to his side, breaking their union, and pulled her into his arms. "I didn't want to crush you."

Because of the baby. Now she got it. Somehow Jessie had forgotten she was pregnant. Not surprising really. Once Jake had put his mouth on her, she'd forgotten her own name.

Jessie stroked her hand over his chest, combing her fingers through the sprinkling of hair. "I don't want you to get a big head, but now I know what all the fuss is about. Thanks for giving me that."

She felt his muscles tense slightly. He didn't look at her, though. He brushed his lips over her forehead. "That was your first?"

"You bet. I would have remembered if I'd had another one of those."

He cursed softly. "No wonder you gave up on men."

Jessie had to agree with him. If she'd known a man could give her *that,* she might have tried again. Or maybe *that* only happened with the right man. A sexual catch-22. In her case, the right man was the wrong one.

He grasped the thick duvet and pulled it over them. She wasn't cold despite only wearing her stockings. The heat from his body was more than enough to keep her warm.

"You're not planning to move to the sofa, are you?" she asked.

"Not unless you want me to."

Jessie shook her head, letting his chest hair tickle her cheek. "I want us to stay in the same bed. But, uh, could you take off your pants? I like the idea of sleeping naked with you."

"Naked." Not really a question, but there was some tension to his voice. A sound rumbled in his chest and he somehow got the pants off without breaking the hold he had on her.

Jessie wiggled to get even closer. She could feel his strong muscled legs against hers. And his stomach. And everything else that made him a man. She might never get to sleep with all these distractions, but that didn't matter. These were precious, stolen moments that she would remember for the rest of her life.

Moments that would end all too soon.

After the breakfast, she'd tell Jake why she had really been working at the cantina. And, of course, everything would change.

Everything.

Chapter Sixteen

Jessie had never dressed side by side with a man before. All in all, it was darn distracting. She slipped into the mist-colored dress that Willa had ordered for her, but she couldn't keep her gaze off Jake. Jake tucking in his crisp white shirt. Jake zipping up his slacks. Jake just brushing his teeth.

It was hard to look at him without her mouth watering. Apparently the activities from the night before had affected her brain. She wondered if it was permanent.

"We'll go back to the ranch after we're done here this morning?" she asked, forcing herself to finish dressing.

"Yes. I think we've accomplished what we set out to do."

And then some. Making love with him was a bonus she hadn't expected or deserved. Too bad it would probably never happen again. He'd kick her out once he found out who she was.

He met her gaze in the mirror. "I want you to stay."

"Here?" Jessie really didn't like that idea. The hotel was beautiful but—

"No, at the ranch."

She shrugged. "Sure, until it's safe for me to leave."

"That's not what I meant. I want you to stay."

It was on the tip of her tongue to ask him how long, but she wasn't sure she wanted to hear the answer. Because she suddenly needed something to do with her hands, Jessie picked up the brush and tried to fix her hair.

"I wouldn't have asked if I wasn't sure," Jake added. He paused and ran his fingertips over her cheek. "Listen, sex is optional. I just want you there, okay?"

The corner of her mouth lifted. "Sex is optional?" she repeated.

Now he smiled. "What I meant is, you don't have to sleep with me just because you're at the ranch."

She touched the handle of the brush to his jaw. "I'll let you in on a little secret, Jake. Sex with you really isn't optional. You do crazy things to me just by being in the same room."

He groaned. It was a sound she'd come to recognize. Sexual frustration. Jessie felt it, too. Unfortunately, there wasn't a lot she could do about it. They were expected at breakfast in less than twenty minutes. Or maybe sooner. The sudden pounding at the door was probably Douglas letting them know it was time to come down.

Jake held her gaze a moment longer before he walked out to answer it. On a weary sigh, Jessie finished brushing her hair.

"Where is she?" she heard someone shout. Not Douglas, but Byron.

Jessie dropped the brush and hurried into the sitting room of the suite. What she saw didn't soothe any of the nerves that had sprung to the surface. Byron looked ready to come unglued. He stood there, fists balled at his side, glaring at Jake. Jake was doing his own share of glaring.

"What's wrong?" she asked. "Byron, why are you here?"

He aimed his finger at Jake. "He used you as bait to draw out the lunatic who kidnapped you."

Jessie shook her head. "You're wrong. Jake did this so I'd be safe."

"That's what I tried to tell him," Jake snarled. "He doesn't agree."

Alarmed at the dangerous look in Byron's eyes, Jessie stepped closer to him. She tried to keep her voice level. "We think the person who kidnapped me planned to murder me and frame Jake. That's why we got engaged, so everyone would know Jake doesn't want me dead."

She watched Byron process that. His eyes calmed a little, but then he shook his head. "And how the hell did you know it would work? Good God, Jessie, I read the newspaper this morning. It said there were nearly three hundred people in that ballroom. Three hundred!" His hands fisted again. "Any one of them could have blown your head off, and you wouldn't have known what hit you."

Jessie started to reach for him, then pulled back her hand. She hated the suspicions she had about Byron, but she couldn't seem to make them go away. "I'm safe, all right?"

"No. The hell it's all right! I want you to end this charade right now. I want you to tell him, everyone, who you really are. *What* you are. That'll stop the

killer—not some pretend engagement to Jake Mc-
Clendon.''

Her heart slammed against her chest. Oh God. She
hadn't intended for Jake to find out this way. Not
like this. ''Byron, it's time for you to leave,'' Jessie
said softly.

Jake's low, threatening voice cut through the silence that followed. ''What does he mean, Jessie?''

She looked pleadingly at Byron, begging him to
leave. He didn't. He kept his stony gaze on her while
he answered Jake.

''She's a cop.''

Jessie slowly turned toward Jake. He pulled back
his shoulders and looked at her as if she were a
stranger. ''I planned to tell you today,'' she whispered. It was so inadequate. And sounded like a total
lie.

A muscle flickered in his jaw. ''A cop.'' He didn't
say anything else. He just stood there and stared at
her.

''I'm on a leave of absence,'' she corrected.

But that didn't seem to matter to Jake. His eyes
turned to blue steel.

''She was working undercover at that cantina,''
Byron continued. ''Jessie didn't want to tell you because it might cost me my job. But she doesn't have
to worry about that because I'm telling the lieutenant
everything.''

She could see the wheels turning in Jake's head
and it didn't take him long to come up with a conclusion about why she'd kept her profession a secret.

''This has to do with Christy Mendoza.''

She nodded and tried to steady her breathing. ''It

wasn't an official investigation. At first I thought you'd covered up her death.''

"Go on," he demanded. Whatever they'd shared the night before—the passion, the emotion—wasn't there now. He was as cold as the sudden chill that went through her.

"Christy was a friend. A close friend. We'd spent time in foster care together when we were younger, and then later on we were roommates. The day she died, she called saying she'd landed a part-time job with a caterer and that she was going out to your ranch. She said she thought you were..." Jessie took another breath. "Attractive. She said she was going to see if she could get something started with you."

"Sex," Byron bluntly provided. "Christy wanted to see if she could get you into bed."

Jake shook his head. "She didn't even speak to me, and I damn sure didn't have sex with her." He paused, his expression growing colder. "But you decided I was guilty. You were looking for some way to pin this on me."

It was the truth and Jessie certainly couldn't deny it. "But then I got to know you, and I realized—"

"And the rest?" Jake snapped. "The kidnapping, the pregnancy. Was that part of your plan, too? Were you the one who set out to bring me down?"

"No. God, no." Jessie felt as if he'd slapped her. She flattened her hand on her chest. "All of that was real and it happened just like I told you. I wouldn't do that to you."

"But you'd lie. You let me take you to bed, and the whole time you knew you were lying to me. How? How could you do that?"

"I wanted to tell you. I planned to tell you. Not

like this." She aimed a narrowed glance at Byron. "Will you please leave now?" But she didn't wait for him to agree. Jessie latched on to his arm and led him to the door. There was a security guard on the other side, so she could only guess that Byron had used his badge to get in.

"I don't want to leave you here with him," Byron insisted.

"It's not your decision." She got the guard's attention. "I want you to escort this man away from here." She pushed Byron into the hall and slammed the door in his face.

"You'll regret this!" Byron yelled.

She already did. She should have told Jake the truth days ago.

"Well?" Jake asked the moment she turned back to him. "How do you plan to explain away your lies?"

"I've already explained it. I thought you were guilty of covering up Christy's death. And because I thought that, there was no way I could go walking up to you and tell you about an unauthorized, undercover investigation."

"So you let me believe you were a cocktail waitress at Ray's Cantina." He shook his head. "Jesus! Did it ever occur to you that I'd be madder than hell when I found out how you'd deceived me?"

"Of course it did. That's why I planned to tell you today."

"Today," he repeated wryly. "How convenient. And would you have found an excuse to keep me in the dark if your friend hadn't let the cat out of the bag?"

"I said I would have told you and I would have."

"Right." He turned and headed for the other room.

Jessie followed him. "It's the truth. God, Jake, I wouldn't have slept with you if I planned to continue this investigation."

He whirled back around so fast that Jessie nearly ran into him. "So when exactly did the investigation end, huh? When I put myself in front of those bullets to save you?" He tapped his head and smiled mockingly. "Or did it end about the time I stripped your clothes off and had sex with you?"

The words stung. But not nearly as much as the bitterness in his tone. "No, it ended about the time I realized how much I care for you."

The words shocked her as much as they obviously shocked him.

"That's bull!" he shouted. "You don't care for me."

She grabbed his arm, but he slung off her grip. "All right, if it makes you feel any better, go ahead and dismiss everything I've said as lies—but what I just told you is the truth."

He squeezed his eyes shut and pressed his hands against the wall. "This is how it's going to work. We'll go to this breakfast together—not for my sake, but in case someone still wants you dead. And after we're done here, that's the last time I want to see you. Got that?"

Jessie shook her head, the full impact of his words hitting her at once. Oh God, she'd ruined everything. This went beyond hurt. Beyond pride. He was throwing her out, removing her from his life. "You can't mean that."

"I do mean it. Every word of it." He angled his

eyes to the front door of the suite. "Have the guard escort you to Douglas and Willa's room. I want you to finish dressing there. I'll make arrangements so security can take you somewhere after breakfast."

Now her pride kicked in. It was the only thing she had left. Jessie lifted her chin and met him eye-to-eye. "I'll make my own arrangements."

And because it was all she could do, she turned and walked out. She didn't get far before she realized what had just happened. She'd lost him. She'd lost Jake. And she also realized something else—she didn't just care for him. She was in love with him. Hopelessly in love with a man who hated her.

JAKE DROPPED ONTO THE SOFA and buried his face in his hands. "Hell," he mumbled under his breath, and the profanity didn't stop there. He ran a string of it together, hoping it would release some of the anger that had knotted his stomach.

It didn't.

Jessie had lied to him! Lied about who she was and about what she wanted from him. Jesus, the woman was conducting a murder investigation. Worse, she thought he had killed her friend.

So what else had she lied about? Jessie had denied there were any more lies, but he just couldn't believe her. Had he been wrong about the baby, too? For days now he'd felt the child was his, but was that a lie, as well? Had he let his feelings for her lull him into believing that?

The door flew open and Douglas stormed in. "All right, what happened?"

Jake didn't even look up at him. He figured from

Douglas's perturbed tone that he'd seen Jessie. "I learned the truth about her."

Douglas stayed quiet at first, then sat in the chair across from Jake. Then he asked, "Jessie was lying?"

"Yes."

"She must have come clean because she knew the game was up." He blew out what sounded like a breath of relief. "So how did you find out, anyway? Did you—"

"Her *friend,* Detective Byron DuCiel, dropped by and told me."

Douglas groaned. "To arrest her? Damn, the publicity will destroy us. I knew it. I just knew this woman was trouble from the first minute I laid eyes on her."

"No," Jake corrected. "DuCiel didn't come to arrest her. Jessie's a cop."

Douglas didn't say anything for several moments. "She's what?"

Jake knew the questions Douglas would have. Hell, *he* still had questions about Jessie, and he'd even spoken to her. "She's investigating Christy Mendoza's death. Apparently, Jessie was friends with this woman and received a call from her the day she died." Jake paused and tried to tamp down some of the anger over Jessie's distrust. He knew he wasn't successful when he heard his own voice. "She thought I killed her and covered it up."

"Damn it!" Douglas sprang from the chair and started to pace. "Is that what she'll tell the press?"

"I don't think so." But Jake immediately shook his head, discounting that possibility. "I don't know what she'll do."

Douglas cursed. It was vicious. "So what does Dr. Lisette's call have to do with any of this?"

Jake slowly looked up, catching Douglas's concerned gaze. "I didn't even know he'd called."

"Last night and again this morning. He says it's important." Douglas handed him the note with the phone number.

"But I was in the room—"

"I had your calls routed through my suite."

Jake was about a hundred percent sure he didn't care for that, but there were few things about this situation that pleased him. It was too bad he hadn't received the doctor's call. It might have interrupted him before he made love to Jessie.

He snatched up the phone and punched in the numbers. "Dr. Lisette," he said, when the man answered. "It's Jake."

"It's good to hear from you. Well, we got lucky."

Thank God. He was due for some good news. Jake just hadn't figured it would come from the doctor. "Lucky? How?"

"I found the lab that did Jessie's test. Fortunately, it was under her own name." Before Jake could ask what test, Dr. Lisette continued. "There was a chorionic villi sampling performed. It's a test used to determine paternity."

Well, that explained why Dr. Radelman had that written on the notepad at his house.

"The lab even had your blood sample that they apparently obtained from Cryogen," Dr. Lisette continued. "I don't know how you feel about it, but I wanted you know that the results match."

Jake didn't have a clue what he meant. "Match what?"

There was a short pause. "Your DNA. This test is very accurate, Jake. You're the baby's father."

He was glad he was sitting down. That would have knocked his feet out from under him. God, of all the lousy timing. Jake clenched his teeth and tried not to take out his frustration on the messenger.

"I'm the father," he repeated. "You're positive?"

"The test has a ninety-nine point nine percent certainty. Of course, we can repeat it if you'd like."

"No." Jake took a deep breath. "Thank you for getting back to me." But he couldn't thank the doctor for delivering this news. Jake couldn't think beyond ending this call.

"No problem. Some people don't want to know this," Dr. Lisette continued. "But I also learned the baby's gender, if you're interested."

Was he interested? Jake didn't know. Right now he didn't know anything. This baby complicated things beyond belief. Still, it was his baby. That was a ninety-nine point nine percent certainty. His child. A baby he'd fathered with a perfect stranger. But not just a stranger. A woman who thought he was a killer.

"Jake?" the doctor prompted. "Are you still there?"

"I'm here. Why don't you save the news of the baby's gender. That's probably something you can tell Jessie when you speak to her."

"The baby's yours?" Douglas asked the moment Jake hung up the phone.

"Yes."

"Well, this damn mess just keeps getting deeper and deeper." He stood and started to pace again. "She'll use this. If she thinks you killed Christy, Jessie will use this pregnancy somehow. She'll go to the press and tell them everything. It'll ruin you and the campaign.''

''I don't see how she could use it. We've already let the press know we're engaged. So what if she tells them she's carrying my baby?'' Jake stumbled over the last two words. Could he ever say that without his heart dropping to his stomach?

''She could tell people you were the one behind this insemination plot,'' Douglas pointed out.

Jessie had already accused him of that in the beginning. Jake didn't think she felt that way any longer. ''That doesn't make sense.''

''It doesn't have to make sense. The scandal alone will be enough to fuel the press and the gossips.''

''Maybe. But I doubt if Jessie would have gone through all of this if all she wanted to do was discredit me. She could have done that by announcing that she was investigating me for Christy Mendoza's death.''

Douglas stopped dead center in front of Jake. His eyes were hot and tight. ''God, Jake, listen to yourself. You defend her even now.''

''I'm just stating the facts.''

''And those are facts that came from a woman who repeatedly lied to you,'' Douglas crisply added.

That brought Jake off the sofa. He cut across the room and poured himself a glass of water. ''I know she lied, damn it! I don't need you to remind me of it.''

Douglas's mouth clenched, and he glanced at his watch. ''This discussion will have to wait. We need to get downstairs. I'll come up with an excuse as to why your fiancée can't join us. Where the hell is

Jessie, anyway? I want the guards to keep an eye on her so she doesn't try anything stupid.''

Jake put down his glass and rubbed his forehead. ''She's in your suite. I told her to go there and finish dressing.''

''When?'' Douglas asked.

''Not long before you came in.''

''Well, she's not there.''

Jake looked sharply at Douglas. ''You're sure?''

''I'm positive. I came here straight from my suite. She wasn't in the hallway, either. I would have seen her.''

Jake hadn't thought the morning could get any worse, but that did it. The only thing worse than finding out she was a liar was learning that she was missing. ''She better not have left the hotel.''

''I'm sure she didn't. I doubt she'd want to get too far away from you, especially if she thinks she can convince you to forgive and forget. She's probably off somewhere planning her next move. I'll have the guards look for her. In the meantime, you have a speech to make and you've kept everyone waiting long enough. Finish dressing so we can get downstairs.''

Jake wasn't sure he could put on a calm enough face for this political commitment. Still, there wasn't anything he could do sitting around the hotel room, either. The guards could look for Jessie, while he made his speech. And they needed to find her. Soon. Even if she'd lied about who she was, that didn't mean she was out of danger.

''She's a cop, remember?'' Douglas said, as if reading Jake's mind. ''She can take care of herself.''

Maybe. But he would feel a lot better once he learned where she was.

Chapter Seventeen

Jessie leaned against the wall and closed her eyes. She wouldn't cry. It wouldn't do a darn thing to help the situation. Her insistence, however, didn't stop the tear when it slid down her cheek. Jessie wiped it away, hoping it hadn't left its mark.

She could hear the voices of the people in the banquet room. Someone was testing the microphone. The smell of coffee and fresh pastries seeped into the hallway where she was. There was nothing to indicate Jake's arrival. By her calculations he should have been in there.

But then so should she.

She wouldn't let him down about this, even though it would break her heart to stand next to him, knowing how much he hated her. She'd been so right about how he would feel once he found out the truth. That didn't give her any comfort. She'd finally been right about something. Painfully right.

Something brushed against her shoulder. A touch. Her training and instincts came together at once—this could be the killer and she shouldn't be here unarmed. She spun around and brought up her elbow for a strike to the person's face. But it was Willa. Jessie halted her elbow before it made contact.

"Whoa!" Willa put up her hands defensively. "You're jumpy this morning."

"You have no idea," Jessie mumbled.

Willa struggled several seconds to catch her breath. "What are you doing here, anyway? You're supposed to be in the banquet room. You look awful, you know. And you've been crying. What, did you and Jake have an argument or something?"

"You mean you don't know?"

"Know what?" Willa asked.

Jessie didn't want to be the one to tell her. She'd take the easy way out and leave it for Jake. That way he could put his own slant on events. If he wanted to denounce her as a liar, it was his right to do that.

Willa pulled a small compact out of her purse and dabbed some powder on Jessie's face. "Does this have anything to do with Dr. Lisette's calls?"

That brought Jessie's eyes wide open. "Dr. Lisette? When did he call?"

"This morning and last night. He said he'd tracked down some kind of test results." She finished the makeup repairs and put her compact back into her purse. "What was he talking about, anyway?"

Likely he'd found the results of the paternity test. That was something else Jessie didn't want to discuss with Willa. Actually, it was something she didn't want to think about. Not while she was trying to piece her heart back together.

"I don't know," Jessie lied.

"Well, you'll have to call him back later." She caught Jessie's arm. "Right now we have to go into that banquet room and try to sparkle."

She couldn't sparkle if her life depended on it. "I think they'll just have to settle for me showing up."

"Then, at least try to smile." When Jessie just stared at her, Willa gave her a demonstration. It was a beauty queen's smile, one that had no doubt won her a pageant title or two. "Now, see how easy that was? And I did that with a roaring headache. You might as well get used to it, you know. Jake has at least one or two of these every week. It'll only get more hectic when the election gets closer."

But it would get more hectic without Jessie. After this, she was leaving. "Thanks for trying to help," Jessie told her.

Willa stopped in the doorway that led into the banquet room. She took a deep breath. "When this dog-and-pony show is over, why don't we sit down and try to get to know each other? Then you can tell me all about what a rotten jerk my brother's been."

Jessie shook her head. "He hasn't been a jerk."

Willa kept her gaze on Jessie. "Well, well, I can see it now. I wasn't sure before, but it's written all over your face. You really are in love with Jake."

It would have felt wonderful to deny it, but the lie would have stuck in her throat. "We should go in now," Jessie reminded her, stepping into the room.

"Wonderful," Willa said in a sarcastic whisper. "There's Markham and he's headed straight toward us. Too bad I forgot to bring poison darts with me."

Jessie reminded herself that Markham wouldn't come after her here, in a crowded ballroom, but knowing that didn't do much to stop her heart from pounding. If only there was some evidence to connect him to the plot, then perhaps she could convince the police to bring him in for questioning.

"What's he doing here, anyway?" Jessie asked.

"Since the Citizens' Action Board hasn't made an endorsement yet, they invited both candidates."

Markham stopped just a few inches away from them. He offered Willa a terse greeting before turning to Jessie. "Ms. Barrett, I'd hoped to see you here this morning."

Jessie didn't bother to answer him. Abel Markham didn't deserve even mock politeness from her.

"I did a background check on you," he continued, a smile bending his mouth. "I learned some very interesting things."

"I'll bet. But then, you already knew I worked at Ray's since he's a friend of yours."

"Yes, you were a cocktail waitress. Funny, the press hasn't picked up on that yet."

It wasn't even a veiled threat. The look in his eyes let Jessie know that. "And you'll be the one to let them know," she pointed out.

"Well, of course. I consider it my civic duty." He paused, smiled again. "I'll also let them know about your criminal record." Markham glanced at Willa. "I suppose you know all about that."

Jessie had to give it to Willa. Somehow the woman managed to keep that beauty queen poise in place. "I know many things about my future sister-in-law. And about you," Willa said sweetly. "For instance, I've heard you're an impotent jackass. Any truth to that?"

Markham's smile slipped slightly. "I have proof to back up my claims."

No, he didn't. But he probably thought he did because he'd read the fake rap sheet. Jessie stepped around Markham and Willa.

"It's time I stopped all of this."

Willa caught up with her just before she made it to the podium. "Don't let him provoke you into doing something you'll regret. Think of Jake, of his campaign."

"That's exactly what I'm thinking of. I won't let Markham use me to ruin things for Jake."

Jessie stepped up onto the platform and turned the microphone so she could speak. It took several moments for people to realize she was there, but eventually the conversation began to die down.

"For those of you who don't know, I'm Jessie Barrett and I'm engaged to Jake McClendon. Abel Markham has just informed me that he's spreading rumors. Rumors that he hopes to use to discredit my fiancé. I'm here to set the record straight." She paused when she saw Markham at the back of the room. He didn't look pleased, but he would certainly be even more displeased when she finished. "I'm a police officer on a leave of absence."

That brought on some whispers—whispers that wouldn't stop there. And neither would the confused looks she got from some of the guests. Willa seemed especially shocked.

Jessie cleared her throat. "I've been conducting an unofficial undercover investigation into the death of Christy Mendoza, a woman who drowned at the McClendon ranch. At no time was any other officer involved in this investigation. I acted alone."

The statement just might get Byron off the hook, but she wouldn't know for sure until she returned to Austin to face Lieutenant Davidson. Too bad it had come down to a decision to protect Jake or Byron.

Jake had won out, of course. Not that it would do her much good.

"Why were you investigating that woman's death?" Willa asked. Her eyes were wide and she held her hands stiffly by her side.

Jessie gripped the podium. "I wanted to verify that it had been an accidental drowning and not a suspicious death."

From the back of the room, Markham called out to get her attention. Jessie could tell from the man's expression that he thought he'd just uncovered a gold mine. "So let me get this straight. You, a police officer, believe Jake McClendon had something to do with Ms. Mendoza's death?"

Jessie was about to answer, when a movement caught her eye. She swept her gaze in the direction of the side doors. And there was Jake. Unlike the others, he didn't have a stunned look on his face. There was hate. Just hate.

Jessie had no doubt it was all aimed at her.

JAKE HAD ALREADY STOPPED in his tracks by the time he heard Jessie's last comment. Just seeing her there in front of the group was enough to send his feelings for her on a roller-coaster ride. She shouldn't be up there making herself a target. He wanted to protect her. But then he heard what she said. *I wanted to verify that it had been an accidental drowning and not a suspicious death.*

So she'd told everyone what she should have said to him days ago. It felt like a twist of the knife in his back.

"What does she think she's doing?" Douglas snarled.

He kept his voice at a whisper, but Jake heard the anger in it.

"To hell with this. I'm stopping her."

Jake grabbed his arm. "No, you're not."

"She's trying to ruin you."

It certainly seemed that way, but Jake looked beyond the obvious outcome of this impromptu announcement. The press would have questions about his innocence in Christy Mendoza's death, but that wasn't what concerned him at the moment. If Douglas ran up on that podium and stopped her, the public display would verify the wedge between him and his fiancée. It would give him grounds to kill her. And grounds for her to be killed. After she was done, he would see how much he could do about damage control.

"That investigation is something else I'd like to explain," Jessie continued, her voice trembling. "I've found nothing to indicate that Jake even knew Christy, much less had any part in her death. Hopefully, this will put an end to all the rumors and innuendos. There's no way I could have become involved with a man that I thought was responsible for my friend's death."

Markham didn't speak again until he had nearly everyone's attention. "But how do we know that? I mean, your original suspicions must have been based on something. You had to have seen or felt something to make you believe McClendon was guilty."

Jake watched the emotion cross Jessie's face. Her chin was up, her shoulders straight, but none of that could hide the pain in her eyes.

"As I said, Christy was a close friend and I owed it to her to investigate her death. But I also know

Jake is completely innocent. I'd stake my life on that.''

The room went silent, and Jessie gave an almost apologetic nod before stepping away from the podium.

''Hell. What now?'' Douglas barked. ''Do you want me to get up there and—''

''No,'' Jake interrupted. ''I'll go.''

''You'll tell them that the engagement is a farce?''

''No.'' At all costs, he had to protect the baby. And Jessie.

Jake quickly made his way through the crowd, hoping to stop Jessie before she left. However, by the time he made it to the lectern, she was nowhere in sight. He stepped up, anyway, and took the microphone.

''As you heard my fiancée say, she's a police officer and had been investigating a death. That investigation is over. I'm asking now that you give Jessie and me some privacy when it comes to our personal lives. I'd planned to announce this soon, anyway, but now seems a good time. We're expecting a child.''

That caused the reactions he'd anticipated. There were some stunned looks, some congratulatory smiles, some murmurs. Markham, on the other hand, seemed ready to keel over. Jake searched for Willa and Douglas. They had pretty much the same expression as Markham. This wasn't the way his sister should have learned she'd soon be an aunt. Unfortunately, a killer's plot had made it necessary.

''I know this news will shock some voters,'' Jake continued. ''And all I can say is this pregnancy was obviously unplanned. The baby, however, is very much wanted. Jessie and I are both looking forward to becoming parents.''

Satisfied that he'd done what he could to protect them, Jake stepped down and came face-to-face with his sister. He reached for her, to take her aside so he could explain everything, but she slung off his grip.

''Damn you,'' Willa whispered, her voice tight and filled with anger. As she repeated the words, she turned and stormed down the hall.

Jake considered going after her. But there was nothing he could say that would help her understand why he'd made that announcement. Nothing but the whole truth, and he wasn't ready to tell her that yet. Maybe after the police found the evidence to put Markham behind bars. Maybe after all the danger was behind him. Then he could try to mend bridges with Willa.

Well, he'd made a mess of things. His sister was furious with him. Douglas probably was, too.

And so was Jessie, of course.

Jessie no doubt thought he hated her. He didn't. It'd just been the shock of finding out who and what she really was. A cop. The mother of his child was a cop who'd once thought he had killed someone. She obviously didn't feel that way any longer. She'd risked everything when she made her announcement and declared his innocence. It would probably cost her her job. Yet she'd done it.

For him.

Jessie didn't yet know about the results of the DNA test. She didn't know for a fact the child was his. The news probably wouldn't please her. Right now she might be hoping the baby belonged to anyone *but* him. Heck, she might wish she weren't even pregnant.

The hair prickled on the back of his neck. Jessie wouldn't do something like that. She wouldn't get rid of the baby because of the way she felt about him. Still, it wouldn't hurt for him to go to her and try to talk things out. For the sake of the baby.

Jake immediately shook his head, correcting himself. He didn't want to talk things out just for the sake of the baby. He wanted this for himself. He wanted Jessie.

He only hoped it wasn't too late to convince her of that.

Chapter Eighteen

Jessie inserted her key card and pushed the door open. She had to get her purse and get out of there before Jake or his family saw her. The last thing she wanted to do was face them. Too bad most of her money was at the ranch. Maybe she could convince Byron to help her get it back.

If Byron would speak to her, that is.

After all, she had thrown him out of the hotel suite. And with her announcement in the banquet room, she'd probably done a heck of a lot of damage to his career. It would take some fast talking to persuade the lieutenant that Byron shouldn't be reprimanded for the investigation. It might take a whole lot more than talk to make Byron forgive her for the way she'd treated him.

She hurried to the bedroom and reached for her purse on the dresser. The glint of light that danced across the mirror stopped her hand in mid-reach. It took her a moment to realize what it was. The engagement ring. It occurred to her that she could sell it and use the money for the baby, but she couldn't do that. It would be like taking something from Jake, something that never had really belonged to her.

Jessie took one last look at the ring and slipped it off her finger. She set it next to the cuff links that Jake had worn the night before. A night Jessie would never forget because he'd made love to her.

"Not now," she whispered under her breath. "Don't do this now."

She didn't have time for tears or regrets. There would be plenty of time later for those things. Jessie grabbed her purse and the portable phone from the dresser. She had to call Byron to see if he could help her get out of the hotel. Despite her misgivings about him, she had to trust someone, and he was the most likely candidate.

While she dialed Byron's number, she left the suite and went back into the hallway. She'd walked only a couple of feet when he answered.

"Byron, it's me." Jessie ducked behind a huge potted plant. "Listen, I know I'm probably the last person you'd want to talk to, but I—"

"Right now, you're the only person I want to talk to. Where are you?"

She tried not to feel too much relief. Or have too many doubts. This was her friend, she reminded herself. Her close friend. "Still at the hotel. I'm just outside the room, hiding behind a huge palm plant. I want to get out of here before Jake gets back."

"I can understand why. How can I help? What do you need me to do?"

"I need to meet you somewhere."

He paused. "How about you stay right where you are. I'm walking in that direction right now."

"You're still in the hotel?"

"Yes, and I'm a lot closer than you think. See you in a minute, Jess."

She clicked off the phone and glanced into the hallway. Empty. No Jake. No Markham, either. But then, Abel Markham would be a fool to come after her now that he knew she was a cop. He was probably off somewhere cursing himself for picking the wrong woman for his plot. If she had been simply a cocktail waitress working for Ray, she would probably be dead by now. And Jake would be behind bars for her murder.

Jessie breathed easier when she heard the sound of the metal doors of the elevator. Byron had been right. It hadn't taken him long to get there. She looked into the hallway and saw the man walking straight toward her. Not Byron. *Douglas.* And he looked as if he carried the weight of the world on his shoulders. He had his hands stuffed in his pockets and he was mumbling to himself.

"Something's happened to Jake," he said when he reached her.

She stepped out and felt the blood drain from her head. "What? What's wrong?"

"He's missing. The security people can't find him."

Missing? How could that be? She'd seen him in the banquet room only twenty minutes earlier. "Markham—"

"No one can find him, either." Douglas grimaced and added some harsh profanity. "Damn it, if you know where he is—"

She frantically shook her head. "I have no idea. Have you told the police?"

"Not yet, but I need to do that." He started walking and Jessie followed him.

"If Jake's missing, I want to help find him," she vowed.

He quickened his pace and turned at the end of the hall. "That isn't what Jake would want and you know it. He wants you away from Markham, and since we don't know where he is, the best thing you can do is go back to your suite. I don't want to have to worry about Markham snatching you while I'm trying to find Jake."

Douglas came to an abrupt stop. He whipped out his key card and quickly opened a door. Jessie stepped back. Away from him. But not soon enough. He gripped her shoulder and roughly shoved her inside. Before she could even react, he pulled a gun from his jacket.

Without taking his staked gaze off her, he reached behind him, shut the door and activated the locks. Protectively, she placed her hand over her stomach. It wouldn't help. He had pointed the gun rigged with a silencer right at her. It was then she noticed that he wore a pair of thin surgical gloves.

"One scream," he whispered, "and I'll have to kill you a little sooner than I'd planned."

Her breath caught in her throat. She had faced a gun before in the line of duty, but Douglas didn't just have that weapon aimed at her. He also had it aimed at the baby.

With his other hand, he took out his phone and punched in some numbers. "I have what I promised you," he said to the person on the other end of the line. He turned off the phone and slipped it back into his jacket pocket.

So he wasn't acting alone. He had a partner. Was it Willa? God, was Jake's sister in on this, too?

"Why are you doing this?" Jessie asked. She tried to keep her voice level. No need to give him an additional thrill by letting him see how terrified she was. But she *was* terrified. Not just for herself. And not just for the baby. But for Jake. If he came through that door, there was no telling what Douglas would do.

Douglas shrugged. "For the oldest reason in the world. Greed. Necessary greed," he quickly added. "I need all the money from the trust fund, not just the half Willa will inherit. I have debts to pay."

"That doesn't make sense. Jake will give you the money—"

"Not this much. We're talking millions, an amount that would cause him to ask too many questions."

"Such as?" Jessie wasn't sure she wanted to know, but she needed to keep him talking until she figured out how to get away. It wouldn't be long until his accomplice came through that door. If she could just back up a little farther, maybe she could get into the bedroom before he pulled the trigger.

"I don't want him asking questions about Christy Mendoza's death."

Jessie felt her heart sink. "You killed her. It was you."

He made a sound of superficial agreement. "It was practically an accident, but I couldn't have her telling Willa that I'd tried to have sex with her, now could I?"

"So you killed her, instead."

"Yes. I'm glad I could clear your caseload for you. It must give you some satisfaction to know you've been right about her death not being accidental.''

What she felt wasn't anything close to satisfaction. It was a sickening mixture of fear and hate. Christy had died so Douglas could cover up his indiscretions. It was so senseless. So unnecessary. Douglas had already killed at least once and he probably wouldn't hesitate to kill again. Besides, he had the perfect motive. Millions of dollars.

Douglas obviously intended Jake to take the blame for her death. Even Byron had witnessed Jake and her arguing. He would have to testify about this crazy plot, and God knows how jurors would interpret Jake's involvement in that. Even if he wasn't convicted, he would be in jail because there was no bond for murder. During that time, Douglas and Willa would take control of his estate. And they'd rob him blind.

Jessie eased back a step, but that brought Douglas's aim a little lower. Right at her stomach.

''Don't move,'' he said calmly. ''Remember, I don't want to kill you just yet.''

''And you probably don't really want to shoot me, do you.'' She took a deep breath. ''No, I figure you'll choke me so it looks more like a crime of passion.''

His eyebrow slid up. ''Well, I hadn't thought of it, but you're right. Leave it to a cop to help me with the perfect crime.''

It wasn't a perfect crime that she had in mind. If Douglas had to get close enough to choke her, he would also be close enough for her to fight him off. It would be dangerous since he was a large man, but it certainly beat him shooting her at point-blank range.

"Did you know I was a cop before you had those people kidnap me?" Jessie asked.

"Didn't have a clue. Obviously, I would have chosen someone else. Still, you proved a worthy candidate."

"Lucky me," she mumbled. "And let me guess— you killed Dr. Radelman and the nurse from Cryogen Labs. In other words, you've eliminated everyone who helped you with this plan."

"Their deaths were necessary. So were those of the guards. I couldn't risk leaving witnesses alive. Besides, they entered into this because of greed, because of the money I told them I'd pay for their services. As an officer of the law, I would think, you'd want that kind of scum off the streets."

Jessie shook her head at the sick logic. The man in front of her was the worst scum of all. "With all the money you spent on this plot, you could have paid off your blackmailer."

"Don't I wish. I wrote off the warehouse rental and equipment as campaign expenses. In other words, Jake paid for them. A few diverted campaign contributions paid for the rest. Besides, those costs were paltry compared to what's in the trust fund."

No doubt. The irony made her sick to her stomach. Douglas had used Jake's money to pay for what ultimately resulted in the conception of his child. A child Douglas planned to murder.

"I know what you're thinking," he continued. "Why didn't I just kill Jake and be done with it? I wanted to. I really did. It would have been a helluva lot easier than all of this."

She blinked hard to fend off the dizzy spell. "Then, why didn't you kill him?"

Douglas shook his head. "Jake's will. His estate will go to charity when he dies, and I couldn't very well ask him to change that, now could I?"

"That doesn't make sense. If he goes to jail for killing me, that won't change his will."

"Ah, but then I can get him to change it. I can convince him that Willa will need the money to pay for all of his legal expenses and the upkeep of the ranch. I'm sure he'll give his only sister power of attorney."

So Douglas had it all worked out. Too bad he just might succeed—if she didn't do something. Anything. Jessie could almost hear the seconds ticking off the clock.

"I have a proposition to make," she said.

"You're not in a position to make propositions."

She continued as if he hadn't spoken. "I believe Jake will pay you well if you allow this baby to live. You could hold me somehow, keep me hostage until the baby's born. Then you can kill me."

He gave her an incredulous look. "Do you honestly think I'd keep you hostage for seven months? It'd be a logistic nightmare. I need the money now. And I don't need any questions from Jake."

Jessie jumped on that right away. "Then, make that part of the deal. I think Jake will play by any rules if you tell him the baby will be safe."

"*His* baby." Without taking his gaze off her, Douglas put his ear to the door as if listening for someone. "He knows, by the way. Dr. Lisette found the test results. Jake knows without a doubt that you're carrying his child."

Even if she hadn't had a gun pointed at her, Jessie wouldn't have known how to react to that. Later, if there was a later, she'd give it plenty of thought. Right now she had to bargain with the devil for her life.

"I'm afraid I can't make a deal with you," Douglas concluded. He glanced at his watch. "I can't allow this baby to be born. I need every cent in that trust fund and I don't intend to hand it over to Jake's bastard child."

She lifted her chin. And met his steely gaze head-on. It was the wrong thing to say to her. *The wrong thing.* There was already anger simmering with the fear. That brought it to a full boil. Jessie's eyes narrowed.

"There's only one bastard in this room and it's not my baby."

Douglas squeezed out a hollow laugh. "I suppose you're right. I am a bastard. And I'm about to be a rich one. It won't be long now. No, not long at all."

JAKE WALKED through the suite calling out Jessie's name. No answer. Nothing but the sound of his voice.

Where the hell was she?

He snatched up the phone and called the head of his security team, which was dispersed throughout the hotel. No one on the team had spotted her, and the guards posted at the exits said she hadn't left the building. She apparently wasn't in the suite, either.

Jake searched the bath and the bedroom, and was on his way out when he spotted the ring on the dresser. Jessie's engagement ring. So she had been there, after all. Jake picked it up and stared at it. The fact she'd left the ring told him plenty. She was ending their pretend engagement, ending their association. And he'd been a damn fool not to come after her sooner. He should have begged her not to leave.

"Jessie?" the man called out.

Jake slipped the ring into his pocket and walked back into the sitting room. Byron DuCiel had apparently let himself in. "What do you want?" Jake snapped.

"I'm looking for Jessie."

Jake's first instinct was to toss the man out. After all, it was Byron's tell-all that had caused the rift between Jessie and him. But it wasn't Byron's fault. Jake had needed to hear the truth. He just wished he hadn't reacted like an idiot. If he'd tried to talk things out with Jessie, maybe she'd be here right now.

"I don't know where she is," Jake finally said. "I've got my people looking for her."

"She called me about ten minutes ago."

Jessie had called him? It figured. She trusted her friend beyond reason. Because of that trust, if Byron had anything to do with her disappearance, Jake would personally settle the score.

"Where is she?" Jake asked.

"She said she was in the hallway, hiding behind some plant."

Byron had hardly finished his answer before Jake rushed past him. He hurried up the hallway, looking in every recessed area and behind the plants.

"She said she would wait until I got here," Byron added. "I thought maybe she'd gone into your suite."

"No. But I think she was there earlier." Jake stood in the center of the hallway, his hands on his hips. What now? Where was she? "If she got past security, she might have left the building. Can you think of someplace she might go?''

Byron shook his head. ''I don't think she'd try to make it back to Austin without telling me first. In fact, I don't think she would leave the hotel, especially since she said she'd wait for me here.''

True, and that shook Jake to the core. There were just a couple of reasons why Jessie wouldn't have waited for him. Since he'd made it to the hallway ahead of Byron, perhaps Jessie had seen him and decided to hide elsewhere rather than face him. Or. And it was that *or* that gave Jake the most trouble. Maybe Jessie hadn't had a choice about staying put and waiting. Maybe someone had taken her.

''Hell.'' Jake tipped his eyes to the ceiling and added more profanity. ''Markham might have her.''

''Markham? You think he's the one behind all of this?''

''I think he's the most likely suspect.'' And that was yet another unsettling thought. Everything clearly pointed to Markham. Perhaps too clearly. Was it possible someone had set up the man to make it look as if he was guilty? It might not even matter at this stage of the game. Something might have happened to Jessie.

Not *might*.

Something had happened. Jake could feel it in his soul.

The bell on the elevator clanged once, indicating that someone was about to get off. Jake quickly motioned for Byron to step into the small recessed area between two suite doors. A moment later, the elevator doors slid open and Abel Markham stepped out.

It took some effort for Jake not to storm toward the man and beat the truth out of him. But something told him to stay back. To watch. He was glad he did. Markham rapped once on the suite door nearest the elevator. Obviously, someone had expected him, because in a matter of seconds he disappeared inside.

Jessie was in there, too.

Jake had no proof to back up his theory and didn't need any. He was going in after her. One way or another, he would stop Markham. He only hoped he wasn't too late to save Jessie.

"Do you have a gun?" Jake asked.

Byron took out a pistol from his shoulder harness. "You think we'll need it?"

"Yes." Unfortunately, he did.

JESSIE WASN'T REALLY SURPRISED when Abel Markham came through the door. She'd figured all along that he was in on this. What did surprise her was the astonishment on Markham's face when he saw her. Not just astonishment. Shock.

"What the hell is she doing here?" Markham barked.

As he'd done with her, Douglas reached behind him and relocked the door. Since Jessie had her attention on the gun, she saw the momentary shift Douglas made with his right hand. There wasn't enough time to lunge at him, but it was enough to keep Markham from seeing the weapon. Once the door was locked, however, Douglas raised the gun again.

Markham looked behind him and scowled first at Douglas, then the gun. "I asked what she's doing here."

A brief smile crossed Douglas's mouth. "She's a necessary part of the plan. But then, so are you, Abel."

"Where the hell is my money? You said you had it. So help me God, Harland, if you're messing me around, I'll go to the press and tell them that you killed that woman."

Douglas met Jessie's gaze. "Christy also called her boss that night and told him that I'd gotten a little rough with her when she brushed me off. Ray told Abel, and he made a calculated guess. Of course, I didn't know it was a guess until I'd incriminated myself." He paused. "Obviously, it created a problem. Markham needed money for his campaign and decided to use the adverse situation to blackmail me."

Now Markham smiled.

But for only a split second.

Then Douglas pulled the trigger.

The sound was like a gust of wind. A solid, deadly *swoosh* of air. It took her several seconds to realize she hadn't been hit. But Markham had. A bright red stain was spreading over his pearl-gray suit. With his mouth poised to speak, he collapsed onto the floor in a dead heap.

Jessie didn't bother to scream. She didn't have time for it. She dived over the sofa and huddled behind it. In the same motion she pulled a heavy brass figurine off the table. It was probably useless against a gun, but she wouldn't just let him shoot her without putting up a fight. If Markham wasn't dead, he soon would be. Douglas no doubt intended to come after her next.

"You know, you did me a favor by telling the police about your insemination," Douglas continued.

"This way I can make it look as if Jake killed both of you. Markham, because Jake just couldn't contain his anger against the man who tried to ruin him, and you because he thought you were in on the plan, as well."

There was a mirror on the wall above her. She could easily see Douglas and he was already walking toward her. That also meant he could see her. His eyes, blank and lifeless, seemed frozen. He lifted the gun, took aim.

She gripped the heavy sculpture in her hand and tried to steady her breath. It would be suicide to stay crouched there—Douglas could simply shoot her through the sofa. She had to go on the offensive. *Think.* She had to come up with something. In that moment, Jessie decided that on the count of three she would stand up and hurl the chunk of brass at him. It was a long shot, but it was the only one she had.

"One," she mumbled. Douglas's gaze snared hers in the mirror. And he smiled. Like his eyes, the smile was hollow and cold.

"Two." Jessie shifted her weight so she could bolt in either direction. Even if he shot her, maybe she could manage to hit him. That way, the cops would certainly question him about how he'd gotten the wound.

"Three." She sucked in a hard breath and sprang up. Jessie drew back her hand. She made a headlong leap to the other side of the sofa just as she launched the sculpture at him.

It didn't work.

Douglas dodged it almost effortlessly. And he

didn't miss a step. He came right toward her. The gun still in his hand, and aimed right at her—

Without warning the door flew open, slamming hard against the wall. Jessie caught a glimpse of Byron. And Jake.

Just as Douglas fired.

IT DIDN'T SEEM REAL. Jake prayed it wasn't real. He would take a million nightmares over this any day.

Glass burst out from the mirror, the shards spearing walls and furniture. Jessie yelled something—for him to get down. Douglas shouted, too. A feral roar that was almost inhuman. His voice was a howl mixed with rage.

Jake hadn't expected to see Markham unconscious, maybe dead. And he damn sure hadn't expected to see Douglas like this. Jake didn't ask any questions. He didn't even wait for Byron to react. Jake dived at his brother-in-law, ramming full force into him. They both went to the floor.

The gun. It was Jake's only thought. Get to the gun before Douglas could fire again. He couldn't let him take another shot at Jessie.

Douglas twisted, somehow managing to keep hold of the gun. He pushed the barrel of the weapon right against Jake's heart. For only a moment. However, this wasn't a fight Jake intended to lose. The stakes were too high. Not just a matter of life or death, either. This fight was for Jessie and his child.

Jake managed to shift his weight. Just slightly. But it was enough that he could bring up his forearm. He rammed his fist into Douglas's jaw and his brother-in-law's head flopped back. But the punch didn't incapacitate Douglas. The aim of the gun shifted wildly as Douglas struggled. Jake prayed that if it went off, it didn't go off anywhere in Jessie's direction.

Jake delivered another bone-crushing jolt, and the gun finally scuttled across the floor. He didn't even bother to go after it. He shoved his forearm right against Douglas's throat.

"For Willa's sake, don't make me kill you." The calmness in his own voice surprised Jake. He didn't feel calm. He felt like beating Douglas to a pulp. This man, someone he'd trusted, had nearly cost him everything that was important. Everything. And Jessie was right at the top of that list.

Jessie.

Jake's heart sank. During the struggle he hadn't heard her make a sound. My God, had Douglas managed to shoot her? If so, nothing, nothing would stop him from killing his sister's husband.

"Jessie?" he called out. Even the second that it took her to answer was too long.

"I'm fine. He missed."

And suddenly she was next to him. She even had Douglas's gun in her hands. Byron was there, too, already positioned in a triangular stance, his own gun aimed at the man Jake had pinned to the floor.

He glanced at Markham. God knows what had happened here, but Markham had obviously been a part of it.

"Ease away from him, Jake," Byron instructed. "I want to arrest this sorry excuse for a human being. Who knows, maybe he'll resist and I can blow a freakin' hole in his head."

Jake did get up, making sure that Douglas didn't try to get away. Of course, that would have been hard to do since Byron seemed to want an excuse to kill him. Byron quickly shoved Douglas onto his stomach, had him tuck his hands behind his head and began to read him his rights.

Jessie stepped closer, and Jake circled her with his arms. She was shaking. Not just trembling. He could only imagine the hell she'd been through before he managed to get to her. Soon he'd have her tell him about it. But not now.

Jake led her to the other side of the room. He called his security people, and once they arrived, he scooped up Jessie in his arms.

"Where are you taking me?" she asked.

"Away from all of this."

And since the bedroom was nearby, that's where he went. A few minutes later, he sat on the edge of the bed and held her tightly to him.

"Douglas was the one behind the plot," she finally said.

Jake kissed her to stop her from giving him the details. He couldn't handle those yet. Not when he'd come so close to losing her.

"I don't care if you're a cop," he whispered. "And I don't care who or what you were investigating. All that matters is you're safe and right here where you belong."

"You mean that?" She looked up, measuring him. "I'm in love with you. I don't how it happened."

She made it sound like a miracle. Maybe that's exactly what it was. "I love you, too."

Jessie sucked in her breath. And blinked. "God, I'm probably going to cry again." There was no probably to it. Her eyes watered and a tear spilled down her cheek. "You really mean you love me?

You're not just saying that because we almost got killed?''

"I mean it," Jake assured her. "I love you."

Jessie studied him a moment longer, and when she was apparently satisfied he'd told her the truth, she placed a soft kiss on his mouth. "Then, everything will be all right."

Yes, it would be.

Chapter Nineteen

It was a dream that woke Jessie. Not the nightmare she'd expected to have about Douglas. There wasn't even a hint of the chaos that had gone on the day before at the hotel. No sound of gunshots. No dead body. No questions by the police. The dream was a happy one. In it Jake had made love to her. Much as he'd done when he'd finally taken her to bed at the ranch.

Jessie rolled over expecting to snuggle closer to him. He wasn't there. She was alone in the bed and the balcony doors were open.

Frowning, she threw back the covers and got up. She slipped on a robe, just in case Willa was out there with him.

Jake was there, all right. Alone. Wearing only his boxer shorts and a thin smile. It had rained sometime during the night; the balcony was wet beneath her feet. The air was fresh. Clean.

She walked to him, noticing the worry lines on his forehead. Those lines troubled her. Jake had probably spent hours beating himself up because he hadn't recognized Douglas's plot sooner. She knew that because she'd done pretty much the same thing.

Jake raked his thumb over the sash on her robe. "Why'd you put this on?" There was a suggestion in his tone—he would have preferred her to wear only skimpy underwear. Or nothing.

"I thought Willa might be with you."

He shook his head. "I had her take the sedative Dr. Lisette prescribed. She should be asleep."

"The next few months will be hard on her." It was an understatement. Jessie had seen Willa when she'd been told about her husband and Markham's murder. The woman was devastated. And with reason. Douglas would stand trial for murder and possibly would be given a death sentence. Still, Willa had Jake, and he would no doubt help her get through this.

"So what are you doing out here?" she asked.

He slid an arm around her waist and pulled her against him. "Trying to think about how I should ask you to marry me."

She flexed her eyebrows. "Does that mean you *want* to marry me?"

"That seems the right thing to do. After all, you're carrying my baby. And there's the part about me loving you. Seems as if marriage is the next logical step."

Jessie pretended to give that some thought. Actually, there was nothing to think about. This was exactly what she wanted. "Why don't you just come out and ask me, then?"

He kissed her first. It was long, hard. And, she hoped, just a prelude to things to come. "All right, Jessie. Will you marry to me?"

"Yes, under one condition."

Those worry lines returned. "I've already said I don't mind you being a cop."

"I know. I remember." Jessie was thankful she had a job to return to. Lieutenant Davidson hadn't approved of her methods, but he had been pleased to have Christy's killer behind bars. The lieutenant had decided to give Byron and Jessie only a reprimand, instead of dismissing them.

"Austin's not that far from here," she continued. "And I shouldn't have any problem living at the ranch. Besides, you'll be in Austin a lot yourself after the election."

"Then, what's the condition to you marrying me?"

She took a deep breath. "I don't want you to step in front of any more gunmen for me."

He smiled. "I thought that turned you on."

"No, it scares the devil out of me. I just want something normal for a change. You know, to be in love. Married. Have this baby. Raise it. Maybe have another one in a couple of years."

"You forgot the happily-ever-after part."

"No, I didn't. I want that, too." She buried her face against his neck. The smell of the rain was on him. And something else that she easily recognized. Jake. Just Jake. It was his own unique scent that went straight through her like warm whiskey. "Oh yes, and I want lots and lots of sex."

"Then, we want the same things. Forever. Sex. And all that other stuff, too."

The breeze stirred around them. Jessie stayed quiet, just enjoying the moment.

"Dr. Lisette told me about the baby," Jake whispered.

That brought her head whipping up. "You mean about the DNA test?"

"I'm the father, but I already knew that before he said anything."

He'd dismissed that so easily and had even added a nonchalant shrug. Jake had known. She didn't think it would do any good to ask him how he'd come to that conclusion. Besides, it didn't matter. Not now.

"But Dr. Lisette told me some other things this afternoon when he was here," Jake added.

Slightly alarmed, Jessie pulled back so she could look at him. "What things?"

"Things like the baby is healthy. And he also told me what the baby was."

"You mean, he knows whether it's a boy or a girl?"

Jake nodded. "So do I. Do you want me to tell you?"

It sounded like too big a decision to make at the moment. Her head was still swimming with everything that had happened. "Maybe you'd better save that until I've given it some thought."

"All right. Just let me know if and when you're ready." He kissed her again. Touched her. And slid his hand between them to cup her breast. "By the way, did I mention that I'm in love with you?"

"Several times. I wouldn't mind hearing it again."

"I'm in love with you, Jessie. It's the kind of love that can withstand anything. Now give it right back to me."

She gladly did. It was something she would never tire of saying to him. "I'm in love with you, too, Jake."

Jessie let him lead her in the direction of their

bedroom, but just before they reached the door, she stopped the kiss and looked up at him. Jake knew if they were having a boy or a girl. He actually knew. Did that soft smile on his face mean he was pleased with the news? Or like her, was he just pleased in general about them and the baby?

Suddenly that information seemed like a huge wrapped present that she'd waited all her life to open. And Jessie couldn't wait any longer.

"Okay. Spill it, McClendon. What are we having?"

He didn't answer right away. Jake only smiled in that too leisurely way of his. "I was thinking about the name Elizabeth."

"Elizabeth." The words formed a smile on her mouth. "A daughter."

They were going to have a daughter.

"Good." That was all Jessie could manage. It was hard to speak around the lump in her throat.

"You're right. It's very good."

Yes, it was.

Now it was up to them to make it better.

TRUEBLOOD, TEXAS

Coming in February 2002...

HOT ON HIS TRAIL
by
Karen Hughes

Lost:

Her so-called life. After being
sheltered by her mother for years,
Calley Graham hopes to sign on
as a full-time investigator for
Finders Keepers.

Found:

One tough trail boss. Matt Radcliffe
doesn't have time during his cattle drive
for a pesky investigator who insists on
dragging him back to Pinto, Texas.

**But Calley is one determined woman—so she volunteers
as camp cook on Matt's drive, hoping to keep her
job...and maybe the cowboy, too!**

Finders Keepers: bringing families together

HARLEQUIN®
Makes any time special ®

Bestselling Harlequin® author

JUDITH ARNOLD

brings readers a brand-new,
longer-length novel based on her
popular miniseries *The Daddy School*

Somebody's Dad

If any two people should avoid getting
romantically involved with each other, it's
bachelor—and children-phobic!—Brett Stockton
and single mother Sharon Bartell. But neither
can resist the sparks…especially once
The Daddy School is involved.

"Ms. Arnold seasons tender passion with a dusting
of humor to keep us turning those pages."
—*Romantic Times Magazine*

*Look for Somebody's Dad
in February 2002.*

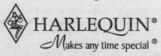

HARLEQUIN®

Makes any time special ®

Visit us at www.eHarlequin.com   PHSD

If you enjoyed what you just read,
then we've got an offer you can't resist!

Take 2 bestselling love stories FREE!

Plus get a FREE surprise gift!

Clip this page and mail it to Harlequin Reader Service®

IN U.S.A.	IN CANADA
3010 Walden Ave.	P.O. Box 609
P.O. Box 1867	Fort Erie, Ontario
Buffalo, N.Y. 14240-1867	L2A 5X3

YES! Please send me 2 free Harlequin Intrigue® novels and my free surprise gift. After receiving them, if I don't wish to receive anymore, I can return the shipping statement marked cancel. If I don't cancel, I will receive 4 brand-new novels each month, before they're available in stores! In the U.S.A., bill me at the bargain price of $3.80 plus 25¢ shipping and handling per book and applicable sales tax, if any*. In Canada, bill me at the bargain price of $4.21 plus 25¢ shipping and handling per book and applicable taxes**. That's the complete price and a savings of at least 10% off the cover prices—what a great deal! I understand that accepting the 2 free books and gift places me under no obligation ever to buy any books. I can always return a shipment and cancel at any time. Even if I never buy another book from Harlequin, the 2 free books and gift are mine to keep forever.

181 HEN DC7U
381 HEN DC7V

Name	(PLEASE PRINT)	
Address	Apt.#	
City	State/Prov.	Zip/Postal Code

* Terms and prices subject to change without notice. Sales tax applicable in N.Y.
** Canadian residents will be charged applicable provincial taxes and GST.
 All orders subject to approval. Offer limited to one per household and not valid to current Harlequin Intrigue® subscribers.
 ® are registered trademarks of Harlequin Enterprises Limited.

INT01